REALMS
OF
LIGHT

OTHER NOVELS BY LAWRENCE WATT-EVANS

Vika's Avenger
The Chromosomal Code
Touched by the Gods
The Rebirth of Wonder
The Nightmare People
One-Eyed Jack
Among the Powers
Shining Steel
(with Esther M. Friesner) *Split Heirs*
(with Carl Parlagreco) *The Spartacus File*

THE ADVENTURES OF TOM DERRINGER
Tom Derringer and the Aluminum Airship
Tom Derringer in the Tunnels of Terror
Tom Derringer and the Steam-Powered Saurians
Tom Derringer and the Electrical Empire

THE CASES OF CARLISLE HSING
Nightside City
Realms of Light

THE FALL OF THE SORCERERS
A Young Man Without Magic
Above His Proper Station

THE ANNALS OF THE CHOSEN
The Wizard Lord
The Ninth Talisman
The Summer Palace

THE OBSIDIAN CHRONICLES
Dragon Weather
The Dragon Society
Dragon Venom

THE LORDS OF DÛS
The Lure of the Basilisk
The Seven Altars of Dûsarra
The Sword of Bheleu
The Book of Silence

LEGENDS OF ETHSHAR
The Misenchanted Sword
With A Single Spell
The Unwilling Warlord
Taking Flight
The Blood of a Dragon
The Spell of the Black Dagger
Night of Madness
Ithanalin's Restoration
The Spriggan Mirror
The Vondish Ambassador
The Unwelcome Warlock
The Sorcerer's Widow
Relics of War
Stone Unturned
Charming Sharra

REALMS OF LIGHT

THE CASES OF CARLISLE HSING, VOLUME 2

LAWRENCE WATT-EVANS

Misenchanted Press

Bainbridge Island

Realms of Light

Published by Misenchanted Press
www.misenchantedpress.com

Cover art by Luca Oleastri—www.rotwangstudio.com
Cover design by Lawrence Watt-Evans

Dedicated to
Edward Bryant,
who accidentally gave me
the clue I needed

Chapter One

I'm a creature of the night, born and raised in eternal darkness—except the darkness on Epimetheus wasn't as eternal as I might have liked. That was why I left Nightside City, where I'd lived my entire life up to then, and came to Prometheus.

And on Prometheus the darkness isn't even close to eternal. What little darkness there is ends every eighteen hours at sunrise, then comes back again at sunset.

What's more, the normal Promethean business hours are during daylight, two days out of every three. Some people go as far as adjusting their circadian rhythms to an eighteen-hour cycle, but most people use a twenty-four hour day, where three days equal four cycles. Office hours come when daylight coincides with the normal waking cycle, on two of those three days.

I didn't like it. I'd had bad experiences with daylight, and didn't care for it much, even when the sun was so small and dim compared to what almost killed me back on Epimetheus.

And this whole optical illusion of the sun moving across the sky made my skin crawl. I knew Eta Cass A wasn't really moving any more than it ever had, that it was the planet's rotation, but that didn't help; it made me dizzy to think about it. I couldn't handle working with the sun overhead, so just about as soon as I'd found myself a residence office I liked I bought a nice piece of software to play receptionist, and figured I'd do my work at night, when everyone else was off. I slept away as many of the daylight hours as I could, and stayed away from windows as much as possible for the rest of them.

At least I'd landed in a city that wasn't right under the moon; I don't think I could have lived with that thing hanging directly above me every time I went out in the open.

A lot of offworlders complained about the earthquakes, but they didn't bother me; we'd had a few on Epimetheus, too. You get used to them. And the lava glow in the distance wasn't any worse than the dawn above the crater rim back home.

The heavier gravity was tiring, and the air smelled strange at first, but I got used to those things, too. There were other ways Prometheus differed from Epimetheus, dozens of them, the algae and the oceans and the rest, but the only one that seriously glitched me was daylight.

One thing hadn't changed. I was still calling myself a detective, a private investigator; it was all I knew. Having office hours that didn't match anybody else's had its good points and bad, in that line of work.

Being on an unfamiliar planet, though—that was all bad for my job. I didn't know my way around the urban software, didn't have any contacts, had no word of mouth bringing in work. I had enough money to live on for awhile—about the only *pleasant* surprise I got when I landed on Prometheus was the lower prices— but I needed an income.

I put notes out on the net, looking for work, of course; I billed myself as an expert consultant on my home world of Epimetheus as well as pitching the investigative work. I talked to some of the software in city hall—this was in Alderstadt, near the north end of Terpsichore in the Nine Islands, which was where my flight in had landed—and tried to learn the circuits.

Strange set-up they had there. The policy software wasn't permanent; every few years they ran a sort of popularity poll called an election, and whoever won got to plug her own software in until the next election. It was something like a referendum, except instead of asking a question they asked you to pick a *person*. And chances were the only names on the ballot were people you didn't even know. Seemed like a stupid system to me, but the people I asked about it argued that it acted as a sort of automatic debugging.

Nightside City always did fine with traditional debugging—you catch a mistake, you rewrite it. You don't pull the whole system offline and put in a new program.

This election thing confused me. What was the point in learning my way around the master program when in a year or two it might get pulled and replaced? It took away some of my incentive, and I didn't really get the hang of Alderstadt city services beyond the basics.

Banks and corporate data and nets are pretty much the same everywhere, though. So are people. I figured I could function, even in Alderstadt.

Then I got my first case, tracking down a data pirate for an off-planet shipping line that picked me because they were in a hurry and my name came up first in a random search. I pulled it off—not as easily as I could have back in Nightside City, but well enough. This artist in margin retailing had figured that knowing what cargos went in and out would give her an edge in pricing, and I found her for the shippers.

When I gave them her name and com code I'd suggested that they just make a deal with her and split her take, but they were having none of it. I got the impression they didn't think much of my morals. Anyway, they got all flashed and turned her in to the Procops, and the whole thing got out on the net.

I figured that wouldn't hurt me any, though it didn't do the margin artist any good and she only missed reconstruction by about half a stop-bit. Yeah, my name hit the net—and it was big enough news that IRC caught it.

The Interstellar Resorts Corporation has been pissed at me for years, ever since I let a welsher skip out, and they put the word out on the net that I was still on their gritlist. IRC isn't as big on Prometheus as they were back home, where the casinos owned about half the planet, but they're big enough that people don't like to annoy them. I'd thought I'd got away from them when I left Epimetheus, but now it looked as if I hadn't.

I was back in the detective business, but I wasn't exactly top of the market. Just like old times.

I got work, though. Sometimes I got people who figured that if IRC was warning them away from me, then that was a point in my favor. I kept eating, and a lot better than I did back in Nightside City, thanks to the lower prices, and I did it without even bleeding my savings, such as they were.

I'd been in Alderstadt for almost a year, gotten myself settled in pretty well, gotten to know the locals, made a few friends, when I got this call. I was there and awake and not doing much of anything, so my software put it through.

"Carlisle Hsing?" a voice asked, and I knew from the sound it was synthesized, which meant I was dealing with software or with someone who wasn't interested in being recognized—and in either case they didn't mind if I knew it. You can synthesize undetectably if you want to pay for it.

"Yeah?" I said, leaning back in my chair—a floater, a nice one. Came with the office. Beat the hell out of the place I'd had back home on Juarez Street.

"I represent someone who wishes to hire your services. Would it suit you to be in the lobby of the Sakai building on First Street in American City at 22:00 tomorrow? Your expenses will be reimbursed."

I reminded myself where in the cycle we were and where on the planet American City was, and figured that 22:00 would be comfortably dark, not to mention well after business hours.

That part sounded all right.

"Do I get a name?" I asked.

"No," it said.

"Then I'll need an advance," I told it. "Buzzfare to American City's gotta be four hundred credits, easy." I was guessing, but since American City wasn't on Terpsichore but on one of the little collateral islands out to the south, it was an easy guess.

"One kilocredit will be posted to your account immediately," it said, without missing a tick.

I smiled. I liked that. I never got this sort of thing back home, and although I'd had a couple of respectable clients in Alderstadt, I wasn't really used to it.

A kilobuck wasn't exactly going to let me retire, or even take a vacation, but it *would* cover round-trip fare to American City, I was pretty sure.

"Any conditions?" I asked.

"You must come alone," it told me. "It would be appreciated if you would allow the installation of a watchdog program in your office com, but this is not an absolute requirement. You must be punctual and discreet."

"No watchdog," I said, and my smile wasn't there any more. This was beginning to sound dangerous. "I'll be there."

"Alone," it reminded me.

"Alone," I agreed.

I meant it, too, if you only counted humans, but I wasn't going to walk into a completely unknown set-up without a little back-up. I intended to have plenty of hardware on me, and of course I carry a symbiote, like everybody else, but mine's a good one, with optional intelligence, and I figured I'd wake it up and have it on the lookout while I was there.

I'd had another symbiote back on Epimetheus, a dumb one. It saved my life and died in the process, so when I got to Prometheus I'd spent a good piece of my savings on getting a better one to replace it.

That was something else that cost about half what it would have on Epimetheus. There were serious advantages to being on a primary colony instead of a secondary one.

"You will be met," the voice said, and then the connection broke.

I sat and I considered that.

Somebody was going to a lot of trouble to deal with me. Somebody in American City, presumably—but I'd never been in American City, never met anyone there, knew nothing about the place beyond the standard stuff in the Prometheography programming I'd jacked in aboard ship.

Why would anybody want me to come to American City?

When somebody wanted to meet me somewhere, it was usually because she wanted privacy—unless it's a closed system, totally closed, anything you do over the com can be tapped, and anyone with any sense knows that. But even so, most people came to my office in that case.

When somebody wanted to meet me somewhere else, it was usually because he was seriously worried or scared, afraid that he's being followed or that *I'm* being watched—and what the hell, maybe I *was* being watched. I wouldn't have put it past IRC to have had an eye on my office, a high-altitude one I couldn't spot, or maybe a bunch of microintelligences reporting back. Or if not IRC, which after all has bigger programs to run, then maybe one of IRC's competitors or subcontractors, trying to figure an angle.

And when somebody insisted on complete anonymity and insisted on meeting me not just outside my office, but in another city a thousand kilometers south of Alderstadt, at the other end of the archipelago, then we're talking about someone who was downright paranoid—or else, just possibly, somebody who was concerned with something other than privacy.

For example, getting me out by myself, alone and relatively defenseless.

Now, I didn't *know* that there was anybody out there who wanted me dead just then, though there had been a few people who might hold grudges. IRC held a grudge, but what I'd done to them wasn't any big spike, really, just a bit of grit.

And there was a fellow back on Epimetheus by the name of Big Jim Mishima who might not be very fond of me—but the exact details got wiped, so he wouldn't know why.

There was that margin player who'd missed reconstruction, but I wouldn't expect her to have the nerve to try anything after a close cut like that.

There were a few people I thought had gone in for reconstruction who might be after me if they hadn't—but I was *sure* that most of them had gone in, and after reconstruction they weren't going to be bothering me, not unless the job had been botched.

There was Sayuri Nakada, a spoiled rich brat I'd crossed up; I didn't know where the hell she was or what she was doing, and she had the juice to be anywhere in human space. I'd probably done her a favor, whether she knew it or not, but she was crazy enough that I had no idea what she thought of me.

So I had potential enemies out there, but I couldn't see that any of them would have been behind this. Mishima was still back on Epimetheus, as far as I knew, and even if he'd gotten off he wasn't the type to come after me without knowing more than he did.

Nakada was petty and vicious enough, but it didn't seem like her style, and besides, she was dependent on the rest of her family, and they wouldn't have allowed it.

If they knew about it.

The thought of the Nakada family beeped somewhere in the back of my brain. I leaned forward and gestured at the com.

The first screen told me that yes, a kilobuck had been credited to my account, from a numbered account at a brokerage house. I could probably trace it back if I had to, but it wouldn't be easy.

The second screen told me that American City was just about where I thought it was, and that Sayuri Nakada no longer had any significant interests there.

But Yoshio Nakada, her great-grandfather, head of the Nakada clan and chief stockholder in Nakada Enterprises, was based there.

Grandfather Nakada knew who I was, all right. He'd paid my way off Epimetheus in return for what I'd learned about a little scam that was being run on great-granddaughter Sayuri. As far as I knew, he had nothing against me, and Sayuri couldn't push him around.

So maybe it wasn't a trap. Maybe Grandfather Nakada wanted to talk to me about something. Certainly he was rich enough to throw kilobucks around like that, and I could see why someone like him wouldn't want to be seen coming to Alderstadt to consult me.

Or maybe it was someone else, lower down in the hierarchy, who had been impressed with my deal with old Yoshio and needed a detective.

Whatever it was, I'd find out soon enough. I'd be there, in the Sakai building at 22:00. I'd be alone—with my Sony-Remington HG-2 loaded and active, with my symbiote on alert, and with every scanner and guard system I could get into my worksuit up and running.

Just in case.

Chapter Two

I buzzed into American City around 18:00, to give myself a little time to look around.

Strange place. Lots of pink glass, detached homes, two- or three-level malls. Bigger than Alderstadt, much bigger; bigger than Nightside City ever was, even before the dawn got too close for comfort.

In Nightside City the Tourist Trap, the central business district, was always ablaze with light, the streets awash in advertising, holos and neon and stardust. It was a constant barrage of color and motion. The streets were always full of people and floaters, despite the wind. The outer parts of the city were darker and quieter, but the Trap never was.

In Alderstadt, the whole city was dark and quiet—at least at night. People stayed inside, maybe because of the cold; floaters were heavily regulated, and nobody advertised more than two stories above street level. Biggest ad I ever saw there wasn't much more than three meters high, a display out front of an exotics restaurant.

I'd gotten used to the low-key approach; my last few years in Nightside I was out in the burbs, and then I'd been in Alderstadt ever since.

American City was the Trap turned inside out. The streets and shells and burbs were blank and silent, but to get anywhere or do anything you had to use the malls, and inside the malls the electronic circus was at full output. The air buzzed with floaters, stardust bloomed above every doorway, holos beckoned on every side, and the walkways were jammed.

Made me feel homesick.

Not that Nightside City ever went in so heavily for pink. That was American City's favorite color, no doubt about it. And of course there wasn't any wind in the malls.

At least the malls were warm.

First Street was malled. I strolled down the right-hand traffic lane watching the displays, admiring the way the floaters picked out the best-dressed people in the crowd for their pitches. That made it pretty clear why some of the really rich people I'd met didn't show it.

The floaters ignored me—I couldn't afford to dress well, and probably wouldn't have bothered to anyway. I got the lightshows, though, and the directional pitches, and the scent traps. There was one place almost lured me in, a neurochemical joint—it wasn't that their own pitch was so great, though the odors were just fine, but I was distracted by a beefcake show across the corner and wasn't paying attention to where I was going. They probably had some sort of subliminals going; I was right at the door when I realized I didn't want to go in.

After that I picked up the pace, and got to the Sakai building around 19:30.

I wasn't there for the meeting yet, I just wanted to scout out the place, see if there really was any chance for an ambush. I figured I'd look it over, get some dinner, look around town a little more, and still be at the meet a few minutes early.

Didn't happen.

I strolled up the black glass corridor between a bughouse and a gene boutique and found the lobby—big room with blue carpet, pink ceiling, and more of the black glass walls. A line of floaters was hanging along one side, right up by the ceiling.

The minute I set foot in the room one of them beeped me—a slick blue and silver one, general purpose, very glossy. The rest ignored me, just hung there, but this one zipped over.

"No names," it said, "I know who you are. You're early."

"Damn it, I'm not here at all," I said. "Not yet." I looked over at the line of floaters; they were shifting a little, closing up the gap my buddy had left.

"Don't confuse me," my glittery little friend said.

"Then don't talk to me," I told it. I turned to go.

It fizzed for a second, then called, "Wait!"

I gave it the three-finger curse. "The hell I will," I said, and started walking.

It followed me. I'd half expected that.

My hand wasn't too far from the butt of the HG-2, but I didn't really have any intention of drawing on the little buzzer. You can't outdraw a floater unless it lets you.

I didn't really have a good reason for being so hostile to the little machine; I just didn't like how little control I had over the situation. It knew who I was; I didn't know a thing about it. It could follow me; if I tried to follow it, it could just sail up out of reach, or probably outrun me on the level. And it could shoot me, if it was armed, but I wouldn't be able to shoot it unless it was ordered to let me, or unless I caught it totally off-guard.

I blew a floater apart once, more or less by both those methods, and it felt pretty good at the time, but I didn't care to try to do it again.

And besides, I didn't really have anything against this one.

Yet.

So I let it follow me, and I didn't say anything. I just walked back out into the mall and down a few storefronts and ducked into a bank.

The human staff was off-duty, but the tellers were up and running, and a few customers were wandering about. One or two glanced up at the floater, but nobody said anything.

I paused and looked about, and reconsidered. Banks are big on security. Not a good choice.

I turned and went back out on the mall, and this time I found a clothier.

"I'd like a private booth," I told the entry clerk. "I need to check some measurements."

It gave me a cheerful little chirp and said, "Certainly, Mis'. We've coded Number Four just for you."

"I'm taking my floater in with me," I told it.

"I'll tell the door," it said. "Catalog's all set on the big screen, any time you're ready."

Damn thing sounded like it was smirking. I hate that sort of smart-chip clerk.

I looked up to be sure Ol' Blue-and-Silver was still there, which it was, and I beckoned for it to follow me, then I marched across the display floor to the fitting rooms.

The door to #4 had a pink stardust aura around it, just to make sure I could find it. It itched a bit when I walked through it; I think my symbiote must have been sensitive to the static field.

The door waited until the floater was inside, then it slid shut. The big holoscreen was showing a montage of models in fancy gowns, any of which would have looked like a tent on me.

"Privacy," I told it. "And kill the display for a moment."

I don't know if it was smarter than the entry clerk, or what, but the room's software didn't say a word, just blanked the screen and lit up an aura around the measuring chip. The screen over the door displayed the word PRIVATE in flowing pink script.

I picked up the chip for the sake of verisimilitude, and then asked the floater, "What the hell were you doing there so early?"

"I could ask you the same question," it said. "I was told to go there and wait for you when I finished my regular duties for the day. I got done at 16:48. Waiting doesn't bother me."

Its tone made it quite clear that it wanted an answer to the question it hadn't actually asked.

"I was checking the place out," I said. "Wanted to see what it was like. I didn't expect anyone to be there waiting for me."

"Shall we return there now?" it asked.

"No," I said.

It thought that over for a second, and then asked, "Why not?"

"Because I don't like that place," I told it. "That line of floaters makes me nervous. Who put 'em all there? Are any of them armed? Look, I wasn't expecting to talk to a floater, and I certainly wasn't expecting to talk to anyone anywhere that public; I figured whoever it was would meet me there and we'd go somewhere else to talk. So I met you, and we came here, and it's still a couple of hours before our appointment, but I'll talk to you here if you want."

"You're being paranoid," it said. "I like that."

"Fine," I said. "Then talk."

"I'm not your client, Hsing," it said. "I don't even know what he wants you for. I was told to meet you and look you over, and if I approved to bring you to him. I've met you and looked you over, and I approve."

"So you're going to take me to him?"

"If you'll come, yes."

"Then let's go," I said.

We went, back to the Sakai Building, and up to the tenth floor.

Then I waited in a lounge, watching waves of green and blue chase each other across the furniture, while the floater went on into the inner sanctum. No holoscreen. No attendant software. No floaters. I sat.

It was maybe ten minutes before the floater reappeared through a holographic wall.

"Hsing," it said, "you'll have to leave your gun."

I didn't say anything for a minute, just stared at it.

"You're not the only one around here who's paranoid," it added helpfully.

"Hell," I said with a shrug. I pulled out the HG-2 and laid it on a table. I considered turning it on, with orders to refuse handling by anyone but me, but decided that was pushing it. It was just a gun. If it got nervous and blew someone's hand off I could catch some serious grit.

I did say, "It better still be here, untouched, when I get back."

"It will be," the floater said.

I wasn't particularly happy about leaving the gun, but it wasn't any great disaster to give it up. I still had plenty of other gadgetry on me.

The big difference—which my mystery man was probably well aware of—was that almost everything else I carried was defensive, rather than offensive. And the rest of my offensive arsenal, such as it was, was relatively easy to defend against, while stopping an armor-piercing round from the Sony-Remington could be a challenge.

Taking the gun and leaving the rest was a pretty fair balance between courtesy and caution on my host's part, and I could live with it.

Then at last I was shown into the other room.

It was a small room, maybe three meters square. The walls were covered with shielding—not built-in stuff, but the heaviest portable shielding I'd ever seen in my life. They weren't passing anything I could see—certainly no visible light, and nothing that registered on any of the pocket equipment I had jacked in. My symbiote wasn't telling me anything, either. The floor and ceiling were shielded, too. I was inside a black box.

Once I was inside the floater extended a grapple and slid shut another panel, closing the box. I was completely sealed off from the outside world. Some of my transponder-based stuff objected; I overrode it.

The only illumination came from the floater, which had stepped itself up from running lights to moderate output and shifted from monochrome to full spectrum; the effect was eerie.

In the box with me were two chairs, two of the strangest chairs I'd ever seen, rigid and angular, and made of a material I didn't identify at first—wood. With seats of some kind of woven string.

They looked, and presumably were, positively ancient. Antiques. Real second-millennium stuff. They looked out of place in that box of shielding.

Sitting on one of the chairs, and the only other thing in there besides the floater, the chairs, and myself, was an old man. A very old man. He went better with the chairs than with the box, but not very well with either one. He wore a simple red robe, and I could see no equipment at all. A dimple under his ear had to be a com jack, but it was camouflaged beautifully. His hair was white and thinning, his face wrinkled—if he'd ever bothered with cosmetic surgery, he was past that point now. No ornamental wiring, no colorants, not so much as an earring.

I'd seen that face before, on the holo and in stills, but I'd never met him before, never spoken with him directly. This was Yoshio Nakada. Grandfather Nakada, head of the Nakada clan, chairman of Nakada Enterprises.

"I am honored, Mis' Nakada," I said, bowing.

"Carlisle Hsing," he said. "Please sit down."

I sat on the other chair; it creaked as it took my weight, and the seat felt rough and unyielding beneath me, not reshaping itself at all, though the woven stuff gave very slightly. It was like sitting on some random object, rather than a chair.

"My floater tells me you are a cautious woman," Nakada said.

I gestured at the shielding. "I see you're a cautious man."

"I need to be," he said, "in my position. Mis' Nakada, last year you became involved with my great-granddaughter Sayuri."

He didn't say it like a question, but I treated it as one.

"Yeah," I said.

"Naturally," he told me, "I had you thoroughly investigated after that."

"Naturally," I agreed. I hadn't really thought about it, and I certainly never noticed any investigation, but it made sense, and he had the resources to do the job right, without buzzing me.

"I would like to ask you a question, though."

I noticed the floater gliding forward, so that it could get a good look at my eyes when I answered whatever it was I was about to be asked. I didn't say anything.

"Have you ever had any contact with any member of my family, other than Sayuri and myself?"

That was not the question I had expected, but it was an easy one.

"Not that I know of," I said.

"Another question, then. Have you ever had any contact with Sayuri other than during that unfortunate affair on Epimetheus?"

"No." I'd have liked to have given a more interesting answer, but the single syllable really covered the whole thing.

"Have you ever before had any contact with *me?*"

"Not directly," I said. "I tried to contact you about Sayuri last year, but I wound up dealing entirely with flunkies." I wondered if he were worried about clones, frauds, mindwipes, or what, that he didn't know himself whether we'd been in touch before.

I wondered if Ziyang Subbha would have resented being called a flunky; I suspected he was pretty high up in Nakada's organization.

"Are you carrying any recording devices or microintelligences?" Nakada asked.

"Yes," I said. I didn't see any point in lying.

He glanced up at the floater.

"She's either telling the truth or she was ready for this," it said.

The old man sighed.

"Life is so complicated," he said, "and there is so little we can trust. Everything we do, there is some way to interfere. Everything we think we know, there is some way it could be faked, or some way it could be changed. Mis' Hsing, you did me a service last year —for reasons of your own, I know, and I would hardly expect otherwise. You did me a service in regard to little Sayuri, and I saw no purpose there beyond the honest and straightforward."

"I did it for the money," I said. I didn't want the old man to think I was some kind of idealist. I have some standards, but I'm no philanthropist.

"Is anything more straightforward?" He almost smiled. "And yet you did not betray our secrets in pursuit of more money; you kept your word. You live a simple life, by my standards, and you have shown yourself to be of use. I have decided to trust you."

"Thanks," I said, not without a hint of sarcasm.

"I need to trust someone," he went on, "and I cannot trust anyone in my family, nor in all my corporation, nor anyone associated with them. I cannot trust anyone who has lived long on Prometheus, for my family and Nakada Enterprises are everywhere here. Even picking someone at random, from all those on this planet, the odds are that she would be tainted. So I have turned to you, an Epimethean and an outcast who has shown herself to be a competent investigator."

"Fine," I said, "so that's why you picked me. So what's this problem that you can't trust anyone with?"

He hesitated, and then said, "Mis' Nakada, someone is trying to kill me."

That was not really very startling, given his position, and I was about to say so when he added, "Someone in my own family, I think."

Chapter Three

This theory was obviously supposed to be a surprise to me, but I didn't really look at it that way.

After all, when you get right down to it, there aren't that many possible motives for murder. Sex, money, revenge, and defective programming are the big ones, and all four of those are likely to get tangled up with family matters, particularly when you're talking about a very big, very rich, and very complicated family like the Nakada clan.

If anyone was going to try to kill Grandfather Nakada, a member of his own family would have both the best reasons and the best chances. And any time anyone's that rich, that powerful, that famous, and that old, he's likely to be a target.

But old Yoshio thought he was surprising me, so I just said, "What makes you think so?"

He frowned.

"Before I tell you any more," he said, "I must first know whether you will work for me to investigate this, to find the assassin."

I wished he hadn't said that, because this all very interesting, even if it wasn't exactly shocking, and I'd wanted to hear more before I turned him down.

But I wasn't going to get the chance.

"I'm sorry, Mis' Nakada," I said, "but I don't think so."

He stared at me silently for a moment, and then blinked, just once, and in a low, hard voice demanded, "Why not?"

Good tone he used there. Gave an impression of hidden strength, and it wasn't a voice you'd expect from an old man. He had to be getting on toward two hundred, but you'd never have known it from the voice.

"Because," I said, "it's too damn dangerous. I'd be out of my depth. You need a major security firm if you want to be protected from assassins. I'm an investigator, I'm not a bodyguard."

"Mis' Hsing," he said, "I'm not looking for a bodyguard. I *have* security people, plenty of them. I even still trust some of them. But none of them is as likely to track down the person—or people— behind the assassination attempt as you are. Their software has almost certainly been corrupted. *All* the software in my entire corporation may be infected. Yours is not. And I know that none of my major competitors, nor any of my family, has bought your services; I cannot be sure whether anyone else has been bought."

I sighed. "That's fine for why *you* want *me*," I said, "since you can't trust anyone local and there aren't many private investigators stupid enough to move into unfamiliar territory the way I did. But there's nothing there about why *I* would want *you*—why I'd want this job, I mean."

"I will pay well, of course," he said, waving a hand in dismissal. "I paid you 492,500 credits for the work you did on Epimetheus, and my life is worth far more to me than my great-granddaughter's reputation. Would two million credits, in addition to expenses, be enough to convince you?"

That was tempting. Two million bucks is a lot of juice, especially on Prometheus. I thought about it for a moment.

"In advance?" I said. "And no limit on expenses?"

He blinked again, slowly and deliberately. "Mis' Hsing," he said, "be realistic about this. The money is not important to me. But if I pay everything up front, you will have no incentive to complete the job. And if I place no limit on your expenses, that would make it even worse."

"What did you have in mind, then?" I asked. I might as well hear his offer, I thought.

"One million credits in advance, to be held in escrow by a bank not affiliated with Nakada Enterprises. A corporate expense account equivalent to that of a junior member of the Board of Directors. Upon completion of the job to *my* satisfaction—no one else's—an additional million credits. And I believe I have some additional incentives to offer."

"Go on," I said.

"If I die, under any circumstances that could conceivably be suspicious, before the payment of your full fee, then your expense account will be terminated immediately, and audited. The second million will be forfeit, and the first million will be distributed by the escrow trustee between yourself and my heirs in whatever fashion the trustee deems reasonable after reading your final report."

I nodded, and got ready to turn the whole deal down, but Nakada wasn't finished.

"Furthermore, I believe you have an older brother, a croupier at the Ginza in Nightside City. Sebastian Hsing, by name. And your father, Guohan Hsing, is currently a permanent resident of Trap Under in Nightside City. A dreamer. A wirehead in a Seventh Heaven dreamtank."

My mouth closed and I listened.

"I have the names right?" he asked.

I nodded. He knew he had the names right.

"I am not threatening them, Mis' Hsing," he said, raising a hand in a gesture that I suppose was intended to calm me down. "I want you on my side, not as an enemy. But you know what's happening in Nightside City now."

I didn't bother to nod again. I knew, and he knew it.

Nightside City was about to fry—and it was doing the biggest business in its hundred and sixty year history as the playground of the Eta Cassiopeia system, as all the tourists crowded in to see the last days. Impending doom really appeals to the thrill-seekers, especially when it's a nice, safe impending doom, not anything that's actually dangerous. The incredibly slow planetary rotation that was carrying Nightside City out onto the dayside was steady and predictable—tourists would have plenty of time to get out.

They were pouring in like data from a wide-open search.

That meant that the casinos and all the rest of the Tourist Trap needed all their best employees.

That meant they weren't letting them leave. Round-trip tickets *to* Epimetheus were selling three for a buck, practically—the casinos wanted customers. But tickets *off* Epimetheus—those were not to be had. At least, not if you were worth keeping. If one of the squatters out in the West End tapped out a ticket somewhere no one would weep, but a croupier like 'Chan—they weren't going to let him go, not while the customers were still coming.

When the business finally burned out they'd let him go—if there were still any ships running. He'd probably wind up paying out his life's savings for a steerage berth on an ore freighter bound out-system. Or he'd rot in the mines out on the nightside.

And my father, down in Trap Under, he was already rotting, plugged into dream central. He had a lifetime contract. Once the city went down, though, would they keep up the maintenance on the wireheads?

I wasn't all that fond of my old man, not after the way he and my mother dumped 'Chan and Ali and me, but I wasn't real happy about the idea of him rotting away literally, physically as well as mentally. And if the maintenance crews checked out, that might be just what would happen.

"I can get them both off-planet, off Epimetheus," Nakada told me. "When I have the assassin, I'll do it."

I stared at him for a moment, that ugly wrinkled old face with the smooth white hair, white as death.

He wasn't going to let me say no. He probably thought he'd already told me too much to let me turn the job down and go home. He was accustomed to getting what he wanted, and he wanted me to take this case.

Which might get me killed. After all, anyone who would try to take out Grandfather Nakada wouldn't hesitate to delete me along the way. In fact, if the would-be killer even found out this meeting had taken place, I was probably dead.

Or old Yoshio might decide to delete me himself, once I'd finished the job—or given up on it. If I knew too much now, how much worse when I'd learned more?

But he had a reputation for dealing fairly with his employees; I'd be safer doing what he asked, *much* safer, than I would be turning him down.

So I had to take it, but if I was going to do that, I was damn well going to get everything I could out of it. The only question was how far I could push, how much I could demand, before he got pissed.

I looked up at the blue and silver floater, hanging there motionless.

"It's recording?" I asked.

Nakada nodded.

"All right, here are my terms," I said, leaning forward. "You put this all on record, and you back it up, and if we make a deal you give me a certified copy. You'll pay me five million credits in advance—five million, not two. You'll cover all my travel and com and medical expenses without question, you'll tell me everything I ask for, you won't hold anything back, you'll give me complete access to all family and corporation records, files, software, and personnel. You'll get my brother Sebastian and my father out of

Nightside City and safely to Prometheus immediately. In exchange, I'll find your assassin and everyone connected with her. You won't interfere with the investigation, no matter who or what I go after. Those are my terms. Take it or leave it."

He sighed. "I'll leave it, if you're serious. I can accept all that— if you make either the money or the rescue of your relatives contingent upon your success."

"The money," I said. "The five million bucks when I deliver, not before."

"All of it," he said.

"All of it," I agreed. "You'll pay my expenses, though."

"I will pay your travel expenses only within the Eta Cass system, unless you can provide me with convincing proof that you need to go elsewhere."

"Done."

"Recorded," said the floater.

I could live with it. I'd get 'Chan and our father out, at least. And if I actually found the would-be killer—well, five million is a *lot* of juice.

I was going to give this an honest try, anyway. If it didn't run, well... I'd been broke before. And I'd have 'Chan and my father out of Nightside City.

"All right," I said, "Now tell me all about it. Someone tried to kill you?"

He told me.

Chapter Four

I had time to think it over on the ride back to Alderstadt.

It was not going to be an easy job. Nakada himself had already done the easy stuff, and it hadn't worked.

The way it scrolled along was this: Someone had turned the old man's own personal com against him, in the Nakada family compound itself. In his own bedroom, in fact. He had been settling down for the night, about to jack in for a nice little dreamscape, when he decided to double-check the program. He'd already read out the schedule once, but on a whim, just a lucky accident, he read it out again.

It was wrong. Instead of a sensible, conservative dream enhancer, the com was running a euthanasia program. If he'd jacked in it would have quietly shut down his autonomic nervous system. And when they found him in the morning it could have been put down to wetware systems failure—old age affecting the brain, his body just giving out on him.

After all, he was two hundred and forty-one years old, he said, and at that age no one was really surprised when even healthy people didn't happen to wake up.

He'd shut the bedroom com off from the rest of the household net immediately, of course, and used his personal implants to analyze the programming. It was clever—the euthanasia program was nested inside a worm that would control the entire unit until he was dead, and would then shut itself down, turn control back to the original program, and set markers so that the com's own everyday internal monitoring would wipe out all trace of the worm and its contents, just as if it were an ordinary bit of gritware that slipped in over the lines. The worm was started in the first place by his regular check of the night's dream schedule.

If he hadn't done the check over again after the worm had been invoked, or if the programmer had set the worm to hide its tracks even while it was actually running, he'd have gone to sleep and never woken up. Sweet and simple.

And it was on his own bedroom com. That com was not on the planetwide nets. It wasn't even on the internal corporate nets that Nakada Enterprises ran. It was only hooked into the family's household net.

So only family members could get at it—in theory.

In practice, both the old man and I knew better than that. The household net wasn't totally closed off; it had links to the top-level corporate net, and that had links to all the rest. All those links were heavily screened and firewalled, though. It would take phenomenal skill and planning to work into that bedroom com from outside the household.

It wasn't impossible, but it came close. That meant the most likely explanation was that someone inside the family compound—which meant either a member of the family or one of their AIs—was responsible.

The next most likely was someone on the top level corporate net at Nakada Enterprises.

And so on, down through all the internal corporate nets to the intercorporate net and finally the public net.

That was from the point of view of opportunity; if you considered motive, then business rivals jumped up the scale—but the family and the corporate insiders at Nakada stayed on it, too.

And if you considered means—who knew? Someone who knew a lot about the old man's personal com habits had designed that little booby-trap, but that didn't mean much.

It could be anybody.

Anybody, Grandfather Nakada thought, except me.

So I was going back to Alderstadt to clean out my office—I was moving to American City for the duration of this case. The trip would give Nakada time to start the disks turning to get 'Chan and my father off Epimetheus. When I got back to American City and saw some proof that they were coming, I'd start to work.

There wasn't really much to clean out. I duped my office software, and left one copy in Alderstadt, took one copy with me. I'd already had my gun with me. I didn't own all that much else, in the way of external hardware—mostly just a set of teacups my mother had left behind when she headed out, and a couple of changes of clothing. The furniture was rented; it stayed.

I hadn't made any close meatspace friends during my stay in Alderstadt. I'd gotten to know some of the local software, and I said hello to some of the neighbors when I saw them. There were a few people I chatted with over tea, and around the corner, at Steranko's, I called Ed the bartender by his first name, but that was about it. No one would be heartbroken if I left. I didn't know if I'd be back or not, so I didn't say any goodbyes.

I was on my way out the door when the com beeped. I wasn't in that big a hurry; I turned and went back and sat down.

"Yeah?" I said.

"Mis' Hsing," said a synthetic voice. "There's a problem."

"Yeah?" I said again.

"Details cannot be given here, but you must return to American City immediately."

"I was planning to," I told whatever it was. There was no visual.

"You must go to where you spoke to the floater."

"Got it," I said, and signed off.

If whoever it was was being that mysterious, I didn't want to ask any more questions. I didn't need to, either. It meant that someone wanted to talk to me in private. Either it was the old man, or one of his flunkies, or else the whole investigation had already been blown. Whoever it was didn't want anything important to get out on the nets.

So it was back to the dressing room.

And a couple of hours later, there I was at the clothier.

"Number Four," I said. "I'm superstitious."

The entry clerk said, "I hope you'll find something you *like* this time, Mis'." I ignored the sarcasm, but decided this time I'd pick up a little something—maybe a video scarf. If I was going to keep meeting here, I wanted to keep my hosts happy by buying a few things. I could even put them on the expense account with a clear conscience.

"We've coded Number Four just for you," the clerk said. "Will you be taking your floater in again?"

I looked up, and there was the blue and silver floater, right behind me.

"Yeah," I said.

"I'll tell the door," the clerk said. "You can go right in."

We went. The stardust still itched. "Privacy," I ordered when we were inside. "And kill the display, I want to think."

The booth obeyed. The screen over the door told me we were private. I turned to the floater. "What's up?" I asked.

"Mis' Yoshio Nakada would like to propose a modification of your agreement."

"No," I said.

It fizzed, then asked, "Don't you want to hear what he's suggesting?"

"No," I said again.

It hung silently for a moment, mulling that one over. With the privacy seal on it couldn't ask anyone else to help it make up its mind, so it had to work the problem out for itself, and the neural net in a floater isn't really made for that sort of decision.

Eventually, though, it said, "I would like to ask you to reconsider."

"I don't intend to modify the deal," I told it, "but we're here, so what the hell, give me the read-out."

That it could handle.

"Mis' Nakada would greatly prefer to pay you the five million credits now, in advance, and to bring Sebastian Hsing and Guohan Hsing from Epimetheus to Prometheus only after the investigation has been completed to Mis' Nakada's satisfaction."

That was all, and I let the silence run for a moment.

"Why?" I asked, finally.

"I'm not sure I should tell you that," it said.

"Then I'm damn sure I won't agree to the change," I replied.

It fizzed again, which could have meant almost anything, and then said, "You know that Mis' Nakada is concerned about the integrity of the corporate software in use by Nakada Enterprises."

"Yeah," I said, with a nod. "So?"

"You are aware that Guohan Hsing is currently, by the terms of his lifetime entertainment and maintenance contract, legally incompetent, and a ward of the Seventh Heaven Neurosurgical Corporation. Legalities aside, he is also in an induced coma and kept comatose but alive by machinery owned and operated by Seventh Heaven."

It paused, but I didn't bother saying anything this time. I just stared at it.

"Removing a properly-contracted ward from the property of Seventh Heaven is not legal, except in a very few exceptional circumstances, none of which appear to apply in this case."

"So?" I said. "Nakada knew that from the start."

The floater ignored my objection. "Sebastian Hsing," it said, "is employed by the Interstellar Resorts Corporation at the Ginza Casino Hotel. IRC has classed him as essential personnel. While he is still technically a free adult, if he chooses to leave his job he will be in breach of contract and subject to a fine of up to one million credits. He has not chosen to leave. Nakada Enterprises is forbidden by city regulations to pay his fine, should he choose to leave; to do so would leave Nakada open to lawsuit for employee piracy, and would have serious extra-legal consequences as well. Nakada could make an offer to buy out his contract, and in fact, such an offer has been made. The offer was refused; IRC is not willing to part with Sebastian Hsing's services at any reasonable price, and to make an offer any higher would surely raise suspicions."

"Go on," I said.

"Are you recording?"

"No," I said, which was a lie, but what the hell.

"I believe that Yoshio Nakada had every intention of circumventing these obstacles. However, he now has reason to believe that the corruption of the corporate software available to him is far more extensive than he had realized when he spoke to you last night."

Last night? I'd been thinking of it as earlier today. Not relevant; I ignored that and asked, "What reason?"

"He is unsure whether he can get Guohan and Sebastian Hsing off Epimetheus safely, given the current means available to him," it said, which did not answer my question.

It shut up, and I stared at it for a moment.

"That's it?" I said at last.

"That's it," it agreed.

"But that's stupid," I protested. "Everything he'd need is on Epimetheus, not in the Nakada family compound. All he has to do is send one message to a trustworthy human on Epimetheus!"

"No," the floater said.

"Why the bloody hell not?" I demanded.

"Because all supposedly-secure corporate communications between Prometheus and Epimetheus have been affected. While he has established that there has been interference, Mis' Nakada is unable to determine the nature or extent of the meddling. He attempted to contact Epimetheus after you left last night, and discovered that he cannot tell whether he is, in fact, speaking to a human on Epimetheus, or to a digital simulation—his usual security tests have been compromised. This was not the case when he made his preparations; something has changed. He suspects that when he met with you, his absence from his usual routines was noted and prompted this action. It now appears that the conspiracy that...the conspiracy he is aware of is more extensive than he thought, and there is literally no one employed by Nakada Enterprises on Epimetheus he feels he can trust with the assignment."

I felt a creeping uneasiness somewhere in my spine.

"It's that bad?" I asked.

"I don't know, Hsing," the floater said, "but Mis' Nakada thinks it is."

The thing's manner had changed; it had gone from formal and every centimeter a machine to its more familiar self. I guessed it was because it was back in its familiar groove, no longer stretching its instructions to the limit and telling me things it hadn't been told to tell me.

"If the conspiracy, or whatever it is, is that extensive, how do I even know he sent *you*?"

"If you agree to continue on his revised terms, he will meet you in person to verify it."

"Fine. How the hell does he expect me to stop it?"

"By finding the parties running it, of course."

I snorted. "Sure, that's all," I said. "Finding the people responsible for infiltrating one of the most powerful corporations in the galaxy, and exposing them—that's easy, right? Hell, maybe it *is* easy, I don't know. I've never tried it." I grinned at the floater. "But you know what must be pretty tricky? Staying alive while I do it. That's got to be tough!"

"But Hsing," it said, "you're good at that."

"Good at what?"

"At staying alive. You're tough, Hsing—people have tried to kill you, IRC tried to break you, but here you are."

"Yeah, right," I said. "The old man's stayed alive six times as long as I have—*he's* the one who's good at it!" I shook my head. "And besides, if he can't get 'Chan and my father off Epimetheus, why should I work for him?"

"For the money?" the floater asked, as I paused for breath.

"No, thanks," I said. "Money's nice, but so's maintaining decent odds of living to enjoy it. No family, no deal. That was what we recorded." I reached up and signaled the privacy seal off; I didn't see that we had anything more to talk about. "Guess I'll be buzzing back to Alderstadt," I said. "Good luck to your boss."

"Hsing, wait," the floater said.

I didn't answer, I just headed for the door of the booth.

"Hsing, *please*," it said. "I'm talking to him now. Could you wait? He may have an offer to make."

"What can he offer?" I asked, my hand on the door.

"Hsing," the floater said, "he does have an offer."

"I don't care," I said.

"You will," it stated flatly.

I hesitated, then turned back.

"All right," I said. "Boot it up. What's the offer?"

"You get an unlimited expense account," it said. "The corporation will pay any fines, bail you out, anything. You investigate the infiltration, conspiracy, whatever it is—on Epimetheus. There has definitely been covert activity there. And while you're there..."

"I get them out myself," I finished.

I stared at the machine while I thought it over, stared at the metal that gleamed pink in the booth's light, and the blue plastic that looked almost as black as the plastic streets of Trap Under.

"You've got a deal," I said at last.

Chapter Five

I'd never seen Epimetheus from space before; when I'd left I hadn't bothered to look.

I looked this time, and decided I hadn't missed much.

The ship I was in was Grandfather Nakada's private yacht; the old man had personally escorted me aboard to hand over command. It had all the luxuries, including a live pilot, just in case the old man wanted something the software couldn't handle. The pilot was a redheaded roundeye, tall, with a face I could live with that wouldn't win any awards, 100% natural as far as I could tell. When I asked, the ship told me his name was Colby Perkins.

Wasn't sure I'd heard it right at first, and since the man himself wandered in just then I asked, "Your name's Pickens?"

"It's Perkins," he told me, blinking those pale blue eyes of his—strange how many colors eyes can come in, but usually don't. "Colby Perkins."

"Perkins," I said. "Got it. I knew someone named Pickens once, wondered if you were any relation."

"No, Mis', it's not the same name at all." He seemed a little uneasy about something, wouldn't keep his eyes on me, but it didn't look serious. Maybe he just wasn't used to passengers.

Or maybe I'm uglier than I thought.

At least he wasn't family to Zar Pickens, who welshed on me back on Epimetheus; I wouldn't want anyone who shared ancestors with that human gritware to be piloting any ship I was on.

Whatever, I didn't need to make him uncomfortable, so I looked out the window, and he went away.

Yes, window. Nakada's yacht had big, fancy windows in the lounge, not just vid or holo. I could watch realtime, direct and live, as we came in across the nightside and headed for the field in Nightside City.

There wasn't much to see. Just a lot of darkness, and a seething mass of silver-gray clouds in a gigantic ring at the storm line. If you get out further and look straight down at the midnight pole the planet must look like a practice target, with the pale slushcap at the pole, and then the dark stone around it, and then the circle of clouds where everything precipitates out of the upper-level air currents, and then dark stone again, and finally the bright line of the dayside at the edge. I suppose there would be occasional pixels of light at the various settlements, too.

I never saw it from that angle, though; we came in low so it was just black and grey, no details anywhere until the lights of Nightside City sparkled on the horizon, and an instant later the light of day spread across behind the city in a long, widening arc like a cadcam construction, hot and golden.

I don't like daylight, so I didn't look any more after that. I let Perkins, or maybe the ship, take us into port, and when we were down I hit the ground. I wanted to move fast. The old familiar gravity made me feel light on my feet, ready to run.

One thing about the Wheeler Drive—it's so fast that I hadn't had time to plan much on the way. I'd taken in some data on Nakada's immediate family, but that was about it. I came out of the port without any very clear idea of just what I was going to do.

I could eat and sleep on the ship, if I wanted to—I'd made sure that was understood. I didn't have to worry about finding somewhere to park myself.

All I had to do was find 'Chan and my father and get them out of there, and if I happened to learn anything about the conspiracy against Grandfather Nakada while the program was running, that was fine and smooth. I was supposed to investigate the conspiracy, sure, but all I really intended to do was take a quick look, because the odds were way the hell up there that the important stuff was back on Prometheus. As far as I was concerned, I'd just come for my family.

So where to start?

My father was in a Seventh Heaven dreamtank somewhere in Trap Under. 'Chan was at the Ginza, working for IRC. Neither one was all that easy to pull loose.

But 'Chan would be faster—all I had to do there was convince him to make a run to the ship, and get him off-planet before IRC stopped us. Once we were off Epimetheus, Nakada could debug whatever IRC might want to do.

My father I had to *find* first. And getting him aboard the ship would be easier without 'Chan trailing along.

That meant starting in Trap Under. Do the hard part first.

I waved, and a cab zipped up, door opening.

I got in, and the cab asked, "Where to, Mis'?"

I didn't have an answer for that right there and ready to run.

Most of Trap Under isn't exactly open to the public; they don't want the tourists wandering in, getting in the way. The tourists are supposed to stay up top, where everyone can skim off their money, not get down there in the maintenance corridors. I couldn't just walk in.

The obvious way into the Seventh Heaven dreamtank was through the Seventh Heaven sales office in Trap Over, wherever it was, but that didn't look as if it was going to work too well—if it were that easy, Nakada could have done it and at least presented me with half the deal. Sure, Nakada was a competitor and I was family —but I wasn't *legally* family any more, not since my parents did the dump on me more than twenty years back, and competitors on

Epimetheus weren't all armed camps. Doing a favor for Grandfather Nakada wasn't unthinkable.

So I wasn't going to be able to do this the easy way. I'd have to get into Trap Under somehow, and either scam or bribe or threaten my way to my father.

I tried to remember where the dreamtank was. I'd never visited it—there's no point in visiting dreamers—but I'd had a pretty good map of Nightside City in my head once.

And I'd lost it. Oh, I still had my natural memory, but I hadn't kept it up, hadn't thought about Trap Under in a year or so, and the old artificial-memory back-up had gotten fried when I took a little unscheduled vacation on the dayside, courtesy of the walking gritware who'd been conning Sayuri Nakada.

But the dreamtanks were mostly right under the casinos, to make it easy for big-time losers to cash out permanently; I remembered that much. And maybe I could beep 'Chan, let him know I was back on Epimetheus for the moment.

So maybe I wasn't going to start with my father after all. Maybe my brother *did* come first.

"The Ginza," I said. "Service entrance."

The cab didn't bother to answer, it just zipped up into traffic, headed for Trap Over. I sat back, thinking, and hoping the cab didn't decide to get chatty.

I hadn't really planned anything out; I had wanted to see the situation first-hand before I hit enter. Now I had to decide what I would run at the Ginza. I looked out the window, hoping for inspiration, but just saw twenty-meter ads for nude dancing at the Jade Club.

There was something oddly comforting about those glimmering holographic ecdysiasts glowing against the dark sky. I couldn't have told you just how they were any different from some of the ads in Alderstadt or American City, but they were. They meant I was *home*.

It was a home I could never live in again, I knew that, but it was still home.

Once we were in the Trap I spotted the Ginza, with its distinctive bronze-green tower and dragon banners, but the cab didn't head for the fancy overhang; I'd told it the service entrance, so it looped around and dived down through the traffic, almost hitting a knot of giggling pedestrians as it veered into a tunnel mouth and jigged its way down.

When the cab finally settled to the plastic flooring I still hadn't debugged anything, but I paid the fare and a fat tip—it was Nakada's money, not mine, and the cab hadn't bothered me—and I got out.

The Ginza's service entrance was one level below the streets—technically, the top level of Trap Under. For all I knew, my father might have been just the other side of a wall, though it was more likely he was somewhere deep down, a hundred meters or more below anywhere open to the public.

I still hadn't come up with anything but the obvious, so I walked up to the door and told it, "I'm here to see one of your employees, Sebastian Hsing. It's family business."

"You know you aren't welcome here, Mis' Hsing."

I should have realized it would recognize me. I'd known from my treatment back on Prometheus that IRC still hadn't forgiven me for my moment of folly a few years back, when I'd given a welsher a chance to get away from them, and of course they'd keep everything in the system up to date. Their software wasn't inclined to be helpful where I was concerned.

"I'm not here to play or solicit customers," I said. "I just need to talk to my brother. It's a private matter."

"Is he expecting you?"

"No," I admitted. "I haven't been able to reach him by com."

I hadn't actually tried, since I assumed IRC was monitoring everything he saw or heard.

"I can give him a message," the door said.

That was probably the best I could hope for, so I said, "Tell him Carlie needs to talk to him about an urgent family matter."

"He will receive the message at his next break."

"I'll wait." Human croupiers only did half-hour shifts—the casino didn't want them getting distracted, thinking about the hot player a few seats down, or when dinner might be, or a full bladder. Even more important, they didn't want them watching enough play to start noticing bias in the equipment, so every table changed staff every thirty minutes, and 'Chan would have ten minutes to play his messages and get a drink and whatever before heading to his next position. I could wait that long.

The door didn't say anything. "Should I wait, Mis'?" the cab asked from behind me.

"No," I told it. I almost started to explain that I didn't know how long I'd be there, but then I remembered it was a cab. It didn't care why.

"Thank you," it said, and then it was gone, swooping away at an acceleration that would have been nasty for a human passenger.

I leaned against the wall by the door; the plastic was warm against my back.

I didn't like that I hadn't done any planning. I should have skimmed background from the nets before I landed. I hadn't because I was used to having the data I needed right there waiting any time I bothered to ask for it, but this time I couldn't trust everything I pulled down. I didn't have my old office com that knew everything about Nightside City anymore. I didn't have my new office com from Alderstadt, either. All I had was the public nets and what I carried with me. I wasn't carrying much, and if Grandfather Nakada was right, I shouldn't believe everything I found on the public nets. So I was scrolling blind, seeing what came up the screen.

As I said, I wasn't really looking for Nakada's conspiracy of assassins. I had to assume that if they'd gotten at the old man's dreamware, they were smart enough to spot anyone who went poking around after them. I was just running my own errands, and keeping all ports open for data about the Nakada clan. If anything beeped, I'd take a look. If it all looked smooth, then I'd go back to Prometheus and work that end.

For now, though, it was all family. With Mis' Perkins waiting for me on the ship I could get 'Chan and our father off-planet without any tickets—if I could get them to the port. 'Chan shouldn't be too much trouble, but pulling a wirehead out of the dreamtanks was another program entirely. The only way I had ever heard of a wirehead coming out of the tank alive was if the cops needed her as a witness—city cops or casino cops, either one. If the wirehead survived, she went back in the tank afterward.

I'd seen vid of a wirehead witness once. She looked like walking gritware, and wanted nothing more than to get back to her dreams. She told them whatever they wanted to hear, so she could get it over with and climb back in the tank, and the whole time her eyes were flipping back and forth, trying not to see boring old reality.

If I did get Dad out, the kindest thing I could do would probably be to plug him into a new dreamtank on Prometheus. If Grandfather Nakada froze at paying for that, I'd call it a medical expense.

I didn't think he'd freeze. The money involved wasn't enough to matter to the Nakadas.

But first I had to get Dad out, and to do that, first I had to *find* him. The location of a particular wirehead was proprietary information, not something Seventh Heaven gave out to anyone who asked—an amazing number of wireheads had left enemies behind who might like a chance to cut a few leads on a particular dreamtank, just for old times' sake. After all, people who had a happy life and a lot of friends in the real world didn't buy the dream in the first place.

'Chan might know something. We might be able to run the family pack on some flunky, even though the law said we weren't family anymore.

The door suddenly said, "I have a message from Sebastian Hsing for Carlisle Hsing."

"I'm Carlisle Hsing," I said. I held up my card where the scan could read it, just in case it had decided to need proof beyond whatever it had used to recognize me before.

'Chan's voice came from the speaker. "I get off after my next table. I can meet you in the employee lounge. This better be important, Carlie."

The door slid open. "Please follow the blue light to the employee lounge, Mis' Hsing," it said in its own voice. "Do not attempt to visit other areas."

"Thank you," I said. You never know whether software's advanced enough to appreciate the niceties, and it doesn't cost to use them.

Beyond the door was a drab corridor that led to a door a dozen meters away; a ball of blue light hovered in the air a few meters in. I followed it in.

It led through the door, which opened ahead of me, then around a corner to the right and down another corridor, then up a ramp to another corridor, but this one had thick red-and-black fixed-color carpet and better-quality doors opening off it. I could hear voices, human ones by the sound, somewhere.

Finally the blue light stopped in front of a door upholstered in red vinyl. The door didn't open for me, and at first I thought something had gone wrong, but there was the light, and it *looked* like a lounge. I pushed on the door with my hand, and it swung inward.

The room beyond was littered with discarded plates and teacups. The red-and-black carpet was the same as in the corridor, but more worn, and with several old, dark stains. One wall shone with the gentle blue of a welcome screen. Two tables and a dozen chairs were randomized; I settled onto a chair, let it fit itself to me, then waved at the screen.

"Public access?" I asked.

"Available," it replied.

"Tell me about Seventh Heaven Neurosurgery," I said.

After all, if I was going to have to wait, I might as well put the time to good use.

Half a dozen images appeared, waiting for me to choose—an ad for their services, a financial statement, customer reviews, and so on. I pointed at a newsy.

At least, I thought it was a newsy, but it was hype. "There are many companies offering neurological services," it told me, "but one stands out from the crowd. The name may be Seventh Heaven, but these dreams are second to none."

It went on to tell me that Seventh Heaven had been around for over a century, and was based on Mars, in Sol System. I asked a question at that, and found out that the operation on Epimetheus was a franchise operated entirely by local talent—they leased the name and the equipment from the parent company.

So when Nightside City fried, what would happen to their tanks? These people didn't even *own* them, and somehow I doubted corporate back on Mars was going to come reclaim them if the locals packed up and left when the sun rose over the crater rim.

The com I was talking to didn't have any data on that, of course. I was trying to decide what I could ask that might be useful when the door opened and 'Chan stepped in. He glanced at the screen, blinked, then looked at me.

"Carlie," he said, "what are you doing here? I thought you were on Prometheus!"

"I was," I said. "I came back."

"You did *what?*"

"I came back."

"Why? Why would you do something stupid like that?"

"Two reasons," I said. "First, I got hired for a job that includes poking around the old place a little. Second, I wanted to get you and Dad off-planet before the sun comes up."

"Me... and *Dad?* Carlie, he's in a tank. You know that."

"Yeah, I know that, but what I *don't* know is what Seventh Heaven's going to do with the tanks when the dawn comes. So I want to transfer him to somewhere on Prometheus."

'Chan stared at me for a minute, and even though he's my brother I couldn't read his expression. "Seventh Heaven?" he asked. "Is that the company's name?"

"Yeah," I said. "You don't remember?"

"I don't *care*," he said. "Carlie, they dumped us, remember? They didn't want us anymore."

"He's still our father. Genetically, if not legally."

"Even assuming he is, which I would not be too sure of, so what? He threw us away. We don't owe him anything."

This time I could see the hurt on 'Chan's face just fine. I'd seen it there before often enough. I'd thought he'd be over it by now, the way I thought I was, but I'd obviously misjudged the situation.

I wasn't going to say that directly, though. Instead I said, "I know. I want to get him out anyway."

He stared at me for a few seconds more before he answered, but eventually he said, "You're more generous than I am. Go ahead, if you want, but it's got nothing to do with me."

"I was hoping you could help me find him."

"Me? You're the detective, Carlie. I'm just a croupier."

"But you know people here. I don't anymore."

"Carlie, I'm glad you're free, and I'm happy to see you again, but I'm under contract to the Ginza. I can't go anywhere or help you with anything if it would interfere with my job."

"That's why I came to get *you* off Epimetheus."

He didn't try to hide his annoyance. "And how were you going to do that? I can't get a ticket."

"You don't need one. I have my own ship."

That got his attention. "The hell you do!"

"Fine, I don't. I have the *use* of a ship. My client owns it, but he's back in American City, and I'm here in Nightside City with his ship and crew, and they're under orders to do what I say. I intend to get you and Dad aboard, then get the hell off Epimetheus for good. Are you coming?"

"Who the fuck *is* your client? Since when do you work for people with that kind of money?"

"Since I moved to Alderstadt," I said. "Sayuri Nakada may not have been happy with me, but some of her friends and family thought I'd done a good job. Good word of mouth means I get work."

"Come on, Carlie. Anyone with his own damn spaceship can do better than *you*! I know you're smart, I know you do an honest job, but you're just a widget. Someone with that kind of money can hire one of the big investigation firms."

It jittered me that my own brother didn't think I had the ram to do what I said, but I kept my temper. "He has reasons to keep this off the nets. *You* come on, 'Chan—you think I'd come in here and tell you this if it weren't true?"

"I don't know, Carlie. It's crazy, and sometimes *you* can be crazy."

"Fine, then, but give me this much—come to the port with me and take a look at the ship yourself. If there's really a ship, and the captain says he'll really get you off-planet, will you come?"

"Of course I will! You think I'm an idiot? I don't want to fry. I saw what you looked like after your little stroll on the dayside; Nightside City's going to be a fucking microwave in a couple of years."

"Then come on to the port with me and I'll show you."

'Chan hesitated, then admitted, "I can't."

I didn't know what he was talking about. I thought he was just being stubborn, playing the big brother who doesn't want his little sister taking charge. "Why not?" I demanded. I remembered that IRC was almost certainly listening, given where we were, so I added, "I'm not asking you to skip out on your contract. Just come out to the port, so you can see I'm not crazy. Then you can come back here, and when I'm ready to go you can buy yourself out, nice and legal."

"I can't," he repeated.

"Why *not?*"

"I'm on call," he said.

"So what?" I didn't see how that was a problem.

"It means I agreed to accept an implant," he explained. "I can't go more than ten minutes from the casino or my legs shut down. I can't go as far as the port to check out your story. And I can't buy out my contract—that was part of the deal, too. Like it or not, I'm here until sunrise."

Chapter Six

I couldn't believe my own brother had been that stupid. "What the hell were you thinking, agreeing to that?" I demanded.

"I was thinking the bonus would be almost enough for my fare off-planet," he answered instantly.

"*Almost* enough," I repeated.

"Yeah, *almost*," he said, and I could see he was getting angry—partly with me, but partly with himself. "I knew they were keeping it just a little short of what I'd need. IRC isn't a charity; they want me to stay here until everything cooks. I figured it would help. I wasn't going anywhere for awhile anyway, so I'd have time to find the rest somehow. I didn't know my kid sister was going to show up with a magic carpet to whisk me off to Prometheus."

"It's a ship, not a magic carpet, and getting you and Dad out of here with it is part of my fee."

"Your fee? What the hell, Carlie—who agreed to that? Whose ship is it? Since when do you take anything but credits?"

"When I don't want the job and the client needs to come up with a way to make me take it anyway," I said. "A way I'm having second thoughts about the more I look at you."

"I didn't *ask* for your help!"

"Neither did Dad. I'm here anyway."

"You can leave any time, then. I'm stuck here until my contract is up. Come back for me when the sun's up."

"The offer isn't good that long. The client wants me *now*, and I wouldn't work until he got you two out of here."

"He's willing to hack off IRC and Sixth...Seventh...the dreamtankers to get you?"

"Yes, he is."

"I hadn't thought my little sister was as special as all that."

I was getting annoyed, but 'Chan had always been able to hack my code, and he was angry enough himself that he didn't mind doing it. "Now you know," I said.

"*I* know it, fine, but who knows it who doesn't mind risking a stay on IRC's blacklist? You never used to operate at that level."

"I told you, I've done all right on Prometheus."

He looked at me, and I could almost see the screen flash. "You said Sayuri Nakada's friends and family—you're working for one of the Nakadas, aren't you?"

"None of your business. I'm here to get you off-planet, not tell you my life story."

"That's it, though, isn't it? And I can guess what the case is, and why they aren't hiring one of the big firms."

That froze me up for half a second; he couldn't possibly know about the rigged dream enhancer, so what did he think was up? "What are you talking about?"

"Someone hired you to investigate Yoshio Nakada's murder, didn't they?"

I stared at him for a moment, then said, "So Grandfather Nakada's been murdered?"

"Of course. Don't try to tell me you didn't know—it must have happened while you were still on Prometheus, and there's no way you could have missed it. The family tried to hush it up, but it's all over the nets. And whoever hired you didn't go to one of the big firms because they don't trust them—they know those people will switch sides and back the highest bidder if the money's big enough, and the killer may be one of the big heirs. *You*, though—you're old-fashioned. You stay bought. Especially when they're paying you with me and Dad."

"Lovely theory, 'Chan," I said, but what I was thinking was that he'd come closer to the truth than I'd wanted.

And it was...*interesting* to know that everyone on Epimetheus thought Grandfather Nakada was dead, that the assassination had been successful. I wasn't sure whether it was going to make my job easier or harder, but it definitely pulled up some new menus.

One was the possibility that he really *was* dead, and that I'd been hired by an actor—I didn't think it could be a simulation; sims aren't that convincing. I could *smell* the old man when we spoke, and we shook hands when he left me on his ship, it wasn't just image and audio.

Maybe an actor with a good makeover...

But why would anyone bother? And how had whoever it was gotten me the run of the old man's yacht?

No, I'd spoken to the real Yoshio Nakada, and he'd still been alive when I left Prometheus.

"I notice you aren't denying it," he said.

"I'm not confirming it, either. I'm trying to figure out how I'm going to get you out of here—you and Dad both."

"You can't."

"I'm not convinced."

"Look, I'm going to have almost enough money when my contract's up—why don't you just leave me here until sunrise, then loan me the difference out of all the fat fees you're collecting?"

"You know better than that. Once the sun is over the rim of the crater the fare off-planet is going to be everything you can afford, no matter how much that is. It'll leave you broke. If I try to contribute, it'll leave *me* broke."

He tried to look as if he didn't agree with me, but it didn't work. He shifted aps.

"You can't get me out, all right? Don't worry about it. Do your job. Get Dad out if you really want to, and if you can, then go back to your magic spaceship and fly back to Alderstadt. I'll be fine. I may be broke when I land on Prometheus, but so what?"

"So I'd prefer you to not be."

"If I break my contract with IRC, I'll be worse than broke. Come back when it's run out."

"I *can't* come back."

"Why not? Make that part of your fee."

I looked around, wondering just where the cams were, and what software would be processing this scene. Then I turned back to my brother.

"Break your contract," I said. "The fine's limited to a million credits, and I can cover that."

He stared at me as if I'd been pixelated. "How did you know that, and where would you get a million credits?"

"My client."

"Well, your client must know that whatever the official fine is, IRC isn't going to be content with that."

I couldn't argue with that—unless 'Chan was under someone's protection, someone like Grandfather Nakada, IRC was likely to be vindictive. I knew that from first-hand experience.

"Why can't you just wait for me? What's the rush?"

I wished I knew who or what would be reviewing the recordings of this conversation, but it seemed a pretty safe bet that Yoshio Nakada wouldn't be on the alert list; after all, if 'Chan was right, everyone in Nightside City thought he was dead, and the old man himself had said he had no reliable communication with anyone on Epimetheus.

"'Chan, I made a deal to get you out as my down payment. I don't start the investigation until you and Dad are on Prometheus. You think my client's willing to wait until sunrise?"

"So put it on hold! Go ahead and do your job, then come back for me."

"You really think I'll be able to find Nakada's killer?"

That stopped him dead.

"Oh," he said. "I assumed...I mean, I thought... I always thought you were pretty good at what you do."

"I'm not bad," I said. "But think about it—someone went after *Yoshio Nakada*. You asked me when I started working for people who have their own ships, and I tried to click past it, but you had a good point. I'm a widget. I'm going to try, I'm going to put in an honest effort, but I'm just an ordinary detective. I can't hack the universe's code. Anyone who could get past Nakada's security can probably hide her tracks well enough that I'll never find her. My client's playing a long shot, hiring me. If that long shot comes in, if I find whoever's behind it, then we're smooth, I get paid and you get a free ride to Prometheus, but 'Chan, what if it doesn't pay off? I can't ask for a fee I haven't earned."

"Well, you could *ask*," he said wryly.

"But I wouldn't get it. But if I get you off Epimetheus *now*, that's my deposit, I can keep that. Get it?"

"I get it," he acknowledged. "And I appreciate the try, Carlie, but it's not going to work. I'm stuck here. Find Dad, take him back to Prometheus with you, do your job, and if you pull it off you can come back for me, and if you can't, hey, I'm no worse off than I was an hour ago."

I sighed. I wasn't ready to give up, but I also saw I wasn't going to convince 'Chan of anything unless I could bring something new to the conversation, something I hadn't thought of yet. "Fine," I said. "Can you help me find Dad?"

He shook his head. "No. I didn't even remember the name of the company. I don't know anything more than you." He glanced at the wall display. "I need to get back to work."

"When do you get off? In case we want to talk."

"Midnight. But I'll probably be too tired to do anything but sleep, and what is there to talk about?"

I grimaced. "Probably nothing," I said, "but I'm keeping an open mind."

"You do that, Carlie." He headed for the door. "And see if you can find out who killed Yoshio Nakada. Do that, and we're all set."

"Yeah. I'll try. Good night, 'Chan."

Then the door closed behind him and I was alone in the break room.

I looked at the wall. The hype for Seventh Heaven was still displayed.

"Locate nearest human-operated office for Seventh Heaven," I said. I thought I'd do better persuading a human to cooperate than software.

The hype vanished, and a map appeared, with directions. I snorted.

Seventh Heaven had an office directly under the Ginza. Very handy for the gamblers whose luck ran out. All I had to do was go back up the service corridor and out into the lower level of the casino, then take an elevator down two stories into Trap Under and follow the signs. I trotted out the door and headed for the casino.

When I reached the turn where I didn't head for the door I'd come in through, a voice said, "You are not authorized beyond this point."

"I'm heading to an office down on B3," I said. "Seventh Heaven Neurosurgery. Nothing to do with IRC or the Ginza." I kept walking.

For an instant, it didn't reply. Then it said, "If you diverge from your announced route, you will be escorted from the premises and risk trespassing charges."

"I love you, too," I said. "I won't diverge."

And I wouldn't. I wasn't giving up on my brother, but I wasn't going to be able to fly him away as easily as I'd hoped. For now, I was going after Dad, and once I had him, I would worry about 'Chan.

I told myself I should also look into this story that Yoshio Nakada was dead. If I could trace it back to its source, that might tell me something useful. I didn't really think I could clean out the conspiracy; I'd told 'Chan the truth about that. I was operating far beyond my specs, and I knew it. Grandfather Nakada must have known it, too, but hiring me hadn't cost him anything he couldn't easily spare, so why not? Play enough long shots, and eventually one of them will come in.

I wondered what other programs the old man was running. Surely, I wasn't the only one.

But whether I was the only one or not, I'd been hired to do a job, and I was going to do my best to do that job.

I wished I had my old office com, in my office out on Juarez; it had all the software I'd need to root through half the data on Epimetheus. I'd brought a selection of my best wares with me from Alderstadt, but that wasn't the same as having the network I'd spent years building up here in Nightside City.

I swung open the door and stepped out onto the casino floor, where a flood of sound and color flashed over me. The slap of cards on felt, the buzz and clatter of a hundred different randomizers, and the hum of voices filled the air. So did glittering visual come-ons of every sort, stardust swirls and images of naked women and flashing holograms of personal cards showing million-credit balances, bouncing balls and playing cards and tropical beaches.

It made me homesick. Oh, Alderstadt and American City had their share of advertising, but it wasn't the same as the Trap— Alderstadt closed down at night, and American City seemed to do everything in pink and silver. Nightside City had its own style. I'd had a glimpse of it during the cab ride from the port, but it hadn't really sunk in the way this view did. The casino was like a miniature version of the view of Trap Over I'd had from my old office.

But I wasn't allowed to diverge from my route, so I couldn't stop and take it in. I couldn't poke around. I kept moving.

As I made my way toward the elevator I wondered what had become of the place on Juarez after I left.

Then I told myself I was being an idiot. I knew what happened to it—nothing. Juarez was in the burbs west of the Trap, and sunlight was already crawling down the western rim of the crater that sheltered the city. Most of the west end was already abandoned and empty. There was no way my old landlord had found another tenant.

I stopped in my tracks as a thought hit me.

There was no way my landlord had found another tenant. My old office would be standing empty. Had he even bothered to change the codes, or clear out my old furniture? That com system I had been missing might still be there. Oh, I'd shut it down when I left, but I hadn't taken the time to wipe it properly; there wasn't much on it I'd cared about enough to make sure it was erased.

That was something I might want to check out while I was in town.

Right now, though, I was headed down into Trap Under to find Seventh Heaven and my father's still-breathing remains. I started walking again, ignoring the floaters that were starting to cluster around me, offering free drinks, or a buy-in bonus for the tables, or discounted admission to the private shows.

The elevator was feeling chatty when I stepped in, but I didn't listen as it started telling me about all the delights Nightside City had to offer. "Down," I said. "Level B3."

The doors closed, and once it heard that I was headed lower the ads changed mood. "Rough night?" the elevator asked. "We've got options—credit on easy terms, service contracts, a dozen ways to get back in the game."

"I'm here on private business," I said. "Shut up."

"Yes, mis'." Then it shut up. Some places the elevators would have kept talking, but the Ginza was a class outfit.

The door opened on a quiet corridor carpeted in a restful shade of blue, with walls that shimmered gently. A display hung in the air, directing me to the Ginza's financial center and personnel offices, an organ broker or two, and Seventh Heaven Neurosurgery. I reached up and tapped that last one, and it turned orange; orange arrows appeared in the carpet, as well.

I followed the arrows, and found my way to a door that showed a scene out of some ancient fantasy, with men and women wearing wisps of pastel gauze as they cavorted amid white marble columns and red and gold tapestries. The name "Seventh Heaven Neurosurgery," in golden letters, drifted through the sky visible between the columns.

I walked up to it; the images faded away, and the door slid open. I stepped through into a sunlit forest glade, and a gentle voice said, "An attendant will be with you shortly. A bench is available to your right."

Ordinarily I don't need to be told where the seats are, but the bench was half-hidden by the images, which covered every available surface. Knowing where to look saved me a second or two. I took a seat.

Birds flitted through the trees, green and red and blue amid the golden sunlight and green leaves. It was pretty, but I wasn't in the mood to enjoy it.

"Seems to me it's bad psychology, doing the waiting room up like this," I said to the room. "Doesn't it remind customers that they can live in whatever setting they want without having the whole thing fed straight into their brains?"

"Oh, no," that soothing voice replied. "These are just images. You can't touch them, or smell them, or taste them, and your options are limited to what's already in memory. They're nowhere near as immersive as the dream experience we offer. A quick sample will demonstrate the difference; just five minutes and you'll see just how unsatisfying these mere images of colored light really are. Shall I set a trial session up for you?"

I shuddered. "No. I'm here on family business, I'm not a customer."

"I see. Here's Mis' Wu to help you."

A handsome young man appeared, striding through the trees toward me, with a unicorn close on his heels. His deep-gray worksuit looked incongruous in that fantasy setting, so I wasn't surprised, when the image skipped slightly as the real Mis' Wu stepped through the projection into the room, to see that he was really wearing exactly that suit.

That skip—you'd think they could avoid that, adjust the image on the fly so that it matched the real man. Maybe they just didn't care about such details; after all, everyone who came here knew perfectly well these trees weren't real, the sunlight wasn't real, the birds and unicorn didn't exist.

In fact, I wondered whether they left that tiny flaw in there deliberately, just to remind you that this *was* a cheap illusion, and they could sell you a much better one.

"May I help you?" Mis' Wu asked, smiling.

I stood up. "I'm looking for Guohan Hsing," I said.

"I'm afraid I don't recognize the name."

"Mis' Hsing is a long-term customer," the office voice said. "He has been with us almost twenty years."

"Ah, that was before my time," Mis' Wu said.

In most businesses, I'd expect a front-office type like this to have the complete client specs somewhere in his own head. For a dreamtank, though, what was the point? Generally once someone bought a permanent contract, the only people who had to worry about her were the techs who maintained the tank and kept the customer's body alive. The salespeople didn't need to know who was stashed away in back.

At least, ordinarily they didn't, but here I was, looking for my father.

"What's your interest in Mis' Hsing?" Wu asked.

"It's a family matter," I said. "I'm his daughter."

Wu frowned.

"At the time of his contracting with us, Mis' Hsing had no children on record," the office said.

I sighed. "He emancipated us," I said. "Genetically, he has three children."

"Legally, he has none."

"This isn't a legal matter; it's a family concern."

"Mis' Wu?" the office said, indicating that it had reached the limits of its programming.

"A family is a legal entity," Wu said.

"A family is *also* a genetic network," I said.

"What do you want with Guohan Hsing?"

"I want to be sure he's all right. Certain...genetic issues have arisen."

"Mis' Hsing is in perfect health," the office said. "His life chamber is functioning properly in every way."

"I'm sure it is," I said, smiling. "But as I say, we have reasons to be concerned about his continued health that have nothing to do with Seventh Heaven's no doubt excellent service."

"Are you saying there's some sort of hereditary defect involved?" Wu asked.

"There might be, yes."

"I believe we test our customers for such things," Wu said.

"Indeed we do," the office agreed.

This was not going as smoothly as I had hoped. I thought for a moment, looking at Wu's manly face, then decided that it might be worth giving the truth a try.

"I'm also concerned," I said, "about what's going to happen to him once the sun's above the crater wall, and Nightside City gets bathed in hard ultraviolet."

"Oh," Wu said. "Well, as you can see, we're safely below the surface here. We'll continue our operations uninterrupted."

"You're sure of that?"

"Of course! We have contracts."

"You won't transfer your clients to Prometheus, or one of the mining colonies?"

"We have no plans to do so. The Eta Cassiopeia division of Seventh Heaven is based right here in Nightside City, in Trap Under, and we expect to stay."

"Do *you*, personally, intend to stay?" I asked.

Wu looked uneasy. "I...haven't decided," he said.

"I don't mean any offense, Mis' Wu, but my brother and sister and I would feel more comfortable if our father was housed on Prometheus, rather than here in Nightside City. We would, of course, be happy to pay the cost of transferring him."

Wu's uneasiness turned to misery. "I'm sorry," he said. "We can't do that."

"Why not?"

"Under the terms of his contract, Seventh Heaven Neurosurgery is Mis' Hsing's legal guardian," he said. "We are obligated to ensure his safety. We cannot entrust it to anyone else."

"Yes?"

"We're only on Epimetheus. We can't take him elsewhere."

"You don't have a branch on Prometheus? Or Cass II, or out-system?"

"I regret to say we do not. *All* our life chambers are right here in Trap Under."

Life chambers—who thought up *that* euphemism for dreamtanks? "Can't you transfer guardianship to us?"

"No, Mis' Hsing, we can't. Our contracts are very firm about that; many of our clients are quite insistent on it. The idea of being passed from hand to hand—they find that very disturbing. Our guardianship is non-transferable."

"But we're his *family!*"

"Legally, you aren't."

"Can't you wake him up and *ask* him if we can move him to Prometheus? I'm sure we can arrange matters with a company in Alderstadt, and do it in such a way that Seventh Heaven doesn't lose any credits."

"The potential liability in a situation like that—no, we can't. We can't wake him without a court order, in any case, and even if we did, he wouldn't be legally competent. We have a contract and legal precedents that say as much."

"I don't believe this," I said. "There must be *some* way he can be moved."

"No, I don't think there is."

I stared at him for a moment, and that handsome face of his seemed much less appealing than it had when he first entered.

"Fine," I said at last. "I'm sure he'll be safe here with you."

"I'm sure he will, Mis' Hsing. Honestly."

"Could we at least get a tissue sample to check for genetic disorders?" I didn't really have any use for one, so far as I knew, but I thought I might as well maintain my cover story.

"I think we can do that. Give us forty-eight hours, and we can bring it to you. Where are you staying?"

I grimaced. "Never mind," I said. "Thank you for your time." I turned to go.

"I'm sorry we couldn't be more help," he called after me as I stepped out of the glade and back into the corridors of Level B3.

"So am I," I said.

Because it didn't mean I wasn't going to get Dad out; it just meant I wasn't going to do it legally or easily.

Chapter Seven

A casino cop was waiting for me in the elevator, ready to escort me out of the Ginza. She didn't seem particularly hostile about it; I wasn't being thrown out, IRC was just keeping an eye on me.

I couldn't blame them. After all, I had tried to steal one of their employees. This wasn't about that welsher years ago; this was about 'Chan. I went peacefully.

As I walked I thought matters over, and wondered whether I really had any business here at all. Mis' Wu and the office AI had seemed pretty confident that they could keep my father alive and well in his tank after the sun rose, and maybe they could. Up until Grandfather Nakada had made his pitch, I'd been perfectly willing to leave Dad in their hands. I tried to remember just why it had seemed so urgent to get him and 'Chan out.

Well, 'Chan—he *did* need to get out. I knew how to do it, too, though I hadn't said so where IRC could hear me. I'd need to do it quickly, and it would leave a mess for Nakada to clean up, but I didn't see that as a real problem.

The need for speed did mean I had to leave it until last.

I had come to Nightside City with three jobs to run—get 'Chan out, get Dad out, and see what I could learn about Nakada's assassin. As I told 'Chan, I hadn't really thought I would get anywhere with that third one, but unless I thought of a better algorithm I had to leave 'Chan until last, and getting my father out wasn't running smooth, so maybe I should take a look at the Nakada case.

'Chan thought Yoshio Nakada was dead. That was interesting. Did everyone on Epimetheus think so? I wanted a com. My wrist terminal didn't have enough screen space for some of what I wanted to do, and I didn't entirely trust the systems on the ship— the ship was Nakada property, and even if it was old Yoshio's personal yacht, that didn't mean his family couldn't have tampered with it. I didn't know exactly what I was going to be doing, but I didn't think it was all going to be stuff I wanted the entire Nakada clan to know.

I tapped for a cab before I was even out the door of the Ginza, and one was waiting for me, door open, when I reached the street. I gave my cop escort a friendly wave, then climbed into the cab and told it, "Juarez."

The old neighborhood had dropped a few bits since I left, and it was easy to see why—sunlight was glinting from the upper floors of the taller buildings, which just looked *wrong.* The streets were mostly empty; I guessed some people had already managed to get off-planet somehow, but that most were crowding over to Eastside, deeper into the shadow of the crater wall.

The door of my old building let me in, no questions asked—as I suspected, the landlord hadn't bothered to wipe my access. After all, I'd left Epimetheus, and why in the galaxy would I ever come back? No reason to worry about me.

But here I was, all the same. I went up the one flight to my office.

It was just as I'd last seen it. I walked in and sat down at my desk, and it was as if I'd never left.

Except I *had* left. I'd wiped most of my files before I left, so I knew I couldn't just plug back in and ride the wire. I'd brought copies of my office software, but I didn't have any of the local updates, and I hadn't kept all the data I'd had when I lived here. I hadn't thought I would ever need it. I could get on the nets, I could function, but I wouldn't have everything I used to have.

On the other hand, I had stuff now I'd never had before. I had some access codes Grandfather Nakada gave me. I had information about how Nakada Enterprises was set up here. And I had a spaceship waiting for me at the port.

I booted up my desk, fed in the software I'd brought with me, and ran a few checks. When I was satisfied, I jacked in and started to dig.

'Chan had been right; the stories about how old Yoshio Nakada had died in his sleep, reportedly on the same night he was actually attacked, were all over the nets, and there were rumors that it hadn't been a natural death. People didn't believe that his symbiotes would have let him die without setting off a dozen alarms.

They didn't know what I knew, that he gave the dream enhancer partial override authority that got it past his defenses. Hell, they didn't know a dream enhancer had anything to do with it; they just didn't believe he could die of natural causes without warning.

And of course, I knew something else no one on Epimetheus knew. I knew that old Nakada was still alive and well.

At least, he had been when I left Prometheus, and if he'd died since then it would be an even bigger story on the nets. Dying twice isn't exactly an everyday event even for the spectacularly rich.

So why did everyone in Nightside City think he was dead?

Because they had been told that he was. A report of his death had been received from American City, back on Prometheus, and it had been verified.

But who had sent that report? Who had verified it? How was it done?

Most importantly, *why* was it done? Why did someone want everyone on Epimetheus to think that Nakada was dead? Who did it benefit, and in what way? The Nakada family holdings in Nightside City weren't that extensive. They did own the New York

—the New York Townhouse Hotel and Gambling Hall—which was a mid-range casino in the Trap, catering to both tourists from off-planet and miners from elsewhere on the dark side of Epimetheus.

But that was most of their property here. They owned some unremarkable real estate, and a few small businesses, but nothing else major.

The New York was managed by a man named Vijay Vo. He had been with the Nakadas forever, and had run the New York since it first opened. He ran it well. There wasn't a hint that he might be involved in a plot to murder his employer; the rumors all seemed to take it for granted that the killers, whoever they were, were all on Prometheus. No one had suggested any local ties—but they didn't know Grandfather Nakada was only dead on Epimetheus. I did.

Was Vo a candidate for my assassin?

I didn't see it. He had been loyal for my entire life and more, he was coming up on an honorable retirement soon, the New York was presumably going to shut down at sunrise—why would Vo suddenly turn on Yoshio?

And how would he benefit from the old man's death? He already had a free hand in running the New York, all the more so since Sayuri Nakada got shipped back to Prometheus.

That brought up a possibility—when Sayuri got sent home, who replaced her as the family's representative on Epimetheus? I didn't know, but I thought it would be easy to find out.

It wasn't quite as simple as I thought. There hadn't been any official announcements. I had to poke around a little.

Officially, no one had. Which did make sense. Sayuri had been sent to Nightside City in the first place largely to keep her out of the way after she'd made a mess of things back on Prometheus, and she had been given control of everything the Nakadas did here *except* the New York, since that was the only thing that really mattered.

The position she had held had been created for her; it wasn't really necessary. Vijay Vo wasn't a Nakada, but he was still capable of running everything here himself.

There had been a few visits by one of Yoshio's granddaughters, though, a woman named Akina Nakada. She was Sayuri's first cousin once removed—not a very close relationship. She seemed to have been responsible for making sure Sayuri hadn't left any awkward programs running, and also for seeing that no one on Epimetheus realized just how stupid Sayuri had been, or why she got called back to Prometheus.

Did *she* gain anything from the reports of Yoshio's death? Nothing very obvious, certainly.

Sayuri herself wasn't mentioned anywhere in connection with the supposed death, and hadn't set foot on Epimetheus in almost a year. She might have been involved in the attempt to kill her great-grandfather—she wasn't clever enough to have done it single-handedly, but she could be part of a conspiracy, perhaps even its instigator—but I couldn't see any reason for her to have sent a false report of his death.

There *wasn't* an obvious beneficiary. I couldn't see any way in which the fake death changed anything in Nightside City. Whether Yoshio Nakada was alive or dead, Vijay Vo ran the New York; whether Yoshio Nakada was alive or dead, Akina Nakada was just the family's troubleshooter, not directly involved in anything of consequence. And Sayuri didn't have anything to do with Nightside City anymore.

So what *did* the alleged death change? It didn't change anything in law enforcement, since it had supposedly taken place on Prometheus and it was officially due to natural causes, and not a murder at all. It didn't change anything financially, so far as I could see. It didn't alter the power structure.

I thought at first that it meant any instructions Yoshio sent would be ignored, and maybe someone wanted to undercut him on Epimetheus, but I quickly realized that was buggy—if instructions got through, even if they weren't believed or obeyed, that would start an investigation and the whole program, whatever it was, would crash. If someone was trying to prevent the old man from intervening on Epimetheus, faking his death was exactly the wrong way to go about it. Using whatever software had faked the death reports to block the incoming orders made *far* more sense.

His *actual* death would have had immense effects, but they would all be back on Prometheus, or in the struggling little colony on Cass II, or in other systems entirely. Nothing obvious would change here on Epimetheus—but so far as I knew, it was only on Epimetheus that he was believed to be dead.

The whole thing was glitched. After all, sooner or later someone from Prometheus who knew Grandfather Nakada was still alive was going to show up and debug the system, so any changes in ownership or control or cash flow would be rebooted. Whatever our mysterious gritware wanted, it had to be something that didn't need to be permanent. I tried to think what that could be, and the screen kept coming up blank.

So I almost missed it. I almost just let it go right past me. Finally, though, a passing mention in one report beeped something, and I realized what would be changed by Yoshio Nakada's death that would not be changed by illness, or a trip out of the Eta Cassiopeia system, or bankruptcy, or anything else. I still didn't see why it could possibly matter, but there was one thing that his death brought about.

It meant that his In-The-Event-Of-Death files were opened.

Anyone in any sort of high-risk occupation maintains ITEOD files, of course—all the secrets that you wouldn't want anyone to know while you're alive, but which you don't want lost if you die.

Everyone who might want you dead, everything you've hidden away that you want your heirs to have, it all goes into the ITEOD files, tucked away behind the most ferocious security possible. Anyone cruising the net who gets too close to the ITEOD files gets warned off; try to touch them and you'll get the most horrific feedback you've ever experienced. Go in on wire, and it's like monsters screaming inside your brain, like blinding light and the stench of death. There are layers of software that hate each other guarding it, competing to keep everyone out. Nobody has ever cracked an ITEOD file.

But when a death is reported and verified, the file is delivered to the city cops and read by both a human and an artificial intelligence. It doesn't all become public, but it all comes out from behind the firewalls and encryption.

Did Yoshio Nakada have something in the ITEOD files in Nightside City, something that someone else wanted a better chance to hack? He undoubtedly had terabytes of juicy goodness in ITEOD files back on Prometheus, or whatever the Promethean equivalent of ITEOD files was—I hadn't happened to have any reason to check out whether cities on Prometheus had the same system Nightside City did, but I guessed there was something similar.

The first question was whether Yoshio Nakada even *had* ITEOD files in Nightside City. He'd never lived here.

But he had visited here, he had business interests here, and he struck me as the kind of person who'd want offsite back-ups, so I was guessing he *did* have something here. And if someone had wanted something in that file, faking the old man's death was probably the best way to get at it.

If that *was* the motive for the bogus reports of his death, then was it the would-be assassin who was responsible for it?

Whoever reported the death must have known about the attempted murder; the supposed death matched the failed assassination perfectly, and I couldn't buy that as mere coincidence. Did that mean the liar was the assassin?

Not necessarily. It might be someone else who had been part of the conspiracy, or it might have been someone who found out after the fact, perhaps while spying on the old man. But it certainly *might* be the same guy.

I began to wonder whether I might actually crack this after all, and earn my five million bucks, and get 'Chan and our father safely off-planet. Tracing back the fake death report might not be possible, since the party responsible would have expected that and would have covered her tracks as well as she possibly could, but if the motive really was something in the ITEOD files—and I couldn't think what else it might be—then I might catch her by checking everyone who had accessed those.

In fact, maybe that was why someone had tried to kill Grandfather Nakada in the first place. Maybe the would-be killer didn't really care one way or the other about the old man's death, but was absolutely desperate to get at something in the files.

That was, I admitted to myself, unlikely, but I couldn't rule it out completely.

This was all lovely in theory, but I didn't yet know whether it had any link to reality. I had some investigating to do, and I did it. This didn't call for anything fancy; there were public lists of who was included.

Sure enough, Yoshio Nakada had established standard ITEOD files here in Nightside City fifty or sixty years ago, and they had been updated regularly whenever he visited, and sometimes by encrypted uploads from Prometheus, as well. Those files were turned over to the city cops about an hour after the report of his death was verified.

I went to take a look at them.

I don't mean I left my old office; I didn't. I was still jacked in to my old desk, dancing the nets on wire, and I went looking for the files on the police nets. I didn't have legal access, but I've never worried much about details like that.

I hadn't made up anything special for this sort of cracking, since ten minutes earlier I hadn't known I was going to be trying it, but I had my standard collection of watchdogs and retrievers, and I put them to work. I cruised the cyberscape around the police nets and launched little exploratory jabs into the cracks and crannies, and at the same time I was scrolling through all the public data, looking for anything that might seem relevant and incidentally keeping some of the cops' software occupied.

I focused most of my attention on that, but at the same time some little corner of my head had already moved on to the next question about the falsified death report. I had a theory as to *why* someone sent it, but I didn't have a clue as to *how*.

Grandfather Nakada's floater back on Prometheus had said the old man didn't trust anyone on his staff in Nightside City anymore, and that he believed his family's software had been seriously compromised. I wondered whether he had actually been in contact with Epimetheus at all. Whoever faked the report of the old man's death had somehow controlled communications between the two planets so completely that nothing and no one contradicted his story; in fact, he'd faked official verification of the original lie.

That shouldn't be possible.

A human being couldn't do it unassisted, I was sure of that; some pretty powerful software would be needed to monitor and control all the communications between Epimetheus and Prometheus well enough to catch any reference to whether Yoshio Nakada was alive or dead. Software that powerful was more likely than not to be an intelligence in its own right.

Maybe there really was a conspiracy here, and maybe some of the conspirators weren't human.

And there I was, with my brain plugged into the nets, my consciousness roaming a domain where software was more at home than we mere mortals, poking into places this theoretical intelligence probably did not want me poking.

I had just had that unpleasant thought when one of my retrievers came buzzing back to me to say that it had found Yoshio Nakada's ITEOD files, including the access records, and was fetching me a copy of everything. I just had to keep it active long enough.

I called my watchdogs in to guard it, let my other retrievers shut down one by one as they reported in, and waited.

And I saw it coming, saw it and felt it and heard it through the synesthetic web link, I even *smelled* it, and tasted smoky copper. Something big and blue-black and screaming was searching for... well, I didn't really know what it was searching for, but my best guess was that my retriever had disturbed it, tripped some sort of warning that had brought this thing swooping down on me. It felt like hot melting velvet as it flashed past me down into the police records, and smelled of vinegar and burning styrene.

Three of my watchdogs just vanished, erased down to the last bit. I erased the retriever myself, to reduce the chances of being traced, and then got the hell out of there. I pulled the plug from the back of my neck and was back in my office on Juarez, sitting in the dark—I hadn't reactivated the walls or lights, only the desk. The windows faced east, and I had them dimmed but not opaque, so I could still see the seething, squirming colors of the Trap, but that was the only light in the room—the desktop had gone dark.

I rebooted the desk and took a look. The retriever had downloaded 93% of Yoshio Nakada's ITEOD files, including the complete access log; the odds were that I had gotten whatever was there that I wanted to get.

There was a *lot* there to get; the desk had partially crashed because it had run out of memory and hadn't been able to swap data offsite fast enough. It would have been fine if I had let it slow down, or if the security had been a bit looser, but I'd been in a hurry.

What the hell was in there, that took that much memory? That desk could hold a dozen human minds without straining, right down to suppressed childhood memories, but Nakada's files had filled every last gigabyte.

If I could have talked to the old man just then I would have had some pretty pointed questions to ask, but he wasn't even on the same planet, and communications between the two were not to be trusted.

I had some other questions I didn't think Nakada could have answered. For one, what was that thing that chased me off? That wasn't standard cop security. That wasn't anything I had ever seen before. I didn't know what it would have done to me if I'd let it, and I didn't want to find out. I'd had hostile software in my brain before, and had no interest in repeating the experience.

Did the cops even know it was there? To have the effect it did that thing must have huge bandwidth; it would be hard to miss. Whoever programmed it hadn't been going for subtlety. But if the cops knew it was there, wouldn't they do something about it?

Had it been prowling the nets at random? Was it guarding the old man's ITEOD file? Had it been looking for me? It might be doing any of those, or it might be something else entirely. Maybe I was just in the wrong place at the wrong time. Maybe it was guarding something else, or chasing someone else. Maybe it was after something else in the police net.

Lots of questions, not enough answers.

I had to admit, though, that it looked as if I was onto something. Whether it really was a conspiracy to murder Yoshio Nakada I didn't know; why anyone would *want* to murder Yoshio Nakada I didn't know.

But I was definitely onto *something*.

Chapter Eight

The access log I'd snagged with Grandfather Nakada's ITEOD files wasn't exactly long, nor was it hugely informative. There were only three entries.

An officer named Hu Xiao had accessed the files under the direction of the court, and had copied portions. A note indicated that the copying was for later analysis, and that Mis' Hu had filed a report of his findings. The report was not available to the public.

An analytical program named Dipsy 3 had accessed the files. What Dipsy had done with them wasn't listed. Dipsy was presumably pointed at the files by the courts, same as Hu was.

And finally, someone using a Nakada Enterprises corporate account had downloaded a complete copy of the files. No further details were included.

That third one—if the faked death had been done to get at the ITEOD files...

Well, no. I couldn't rely on that. Someone might have been subtle and gotten what he was after by cracking Hu's storage, rather than the original the cops had. Or maybe Dipsy had been tagged for it. Or maybe the original Nakada download was legitimate, but then our interplanetary liar had gotten at it somewhere in the corporate nets.

But the third one was worth a look, so I plugged back in and started doing a trace on the account.

I'd expected it to be used by the New York Games Corporation, the subsidiary that ran the casino and most of the other Nakada businesses on Epimetheus, but it wasn't. It was a high-level account for officers of Nakada Enterprises itself, or members of the Nakada family.

I unplugged again and stared at the display on my desk.

This was too easy.

Grandfather Nakada thought a member of his own family had tried to kill him. I had guessed that the motive might be connected with his ITEOD files, and here was someone who might be a member of the Nakada family accessing those ITEOD files.

It couldn't be that simple. I was good at my job, but I wasn't *that* good—or rather, I couldn't believe any Nakada could be that *bad* at covering her tracks. Even that grithead Sayuri would probably have done better than this.

Of course, that assumed there was a *reason* to cover those tracks. Maybe whoever this was hadn't had anything to do with the attempted murder, or the fraudulent reports of Yoshio's death.

It also assumed that I could identify which family member it was. That wasn't a sure thing.

I had looked over the Nakada family tree during the flight from Prometheus, but now I pulled it up and looked again.

Yoshio Nakada was the oldest surviving member of the clan; his two siblings, both younger, were long dead. Yoshio had married three times and sired five children—at least, five he acknowledged —over a period of about a century, ending roughly a hundred years ago. There had been eleven grandchildren, twenty-six great-grandchildren (including my old friend Sayuri), thirty-three great-great-grandchildren, and forty-seven great-great-great grandchildren, so far. I didn't bother counting up the three youngest generations; half of them were just kids, and all of them were so low on the corporate ladder that I couldn't take them seriously as any sort of threat.

A lot of these people were dead, and there were dozens of spouses, ex-spouses, and concubines in the mix, of course.

And then there were the two collateral branches. Yoshio's sister Hinako had one daughter, Narumi, who was childless, twice widowed, and still alive, but at last report was on Earth, not in the Eta Cassiopeia system at all.

The Wheeler Drive could have gotten her here quickly enough, but why would she bother? So far as I knew, she had nothing against her Uncle Yoshio.

Yoshio's brother Masanori had been a little more prolific. He had fathered fifteen children on eight wives before he finally died. There were a couple of hundred descendants on that side, but most of them had no real ties to the corporate clan; in fact, most of them were working for New Bechtel-Rand or ITD or other interstellars, not for Nakada Enterprises at all.

I thought I could safely ignore Narumi and most of Masanori's brood, but that still left quite a crowd. Figuring out which of them had a motive to do in their ancestor would call for some processing. So would figuring out which ones had the capability. Jiggering the old man's personal com with a fatal dream enhancement program wasn't something everyone could do.

I frowned. You didn't need to get in there with your own hands to set that up, but you did need real-time access to the family net, which meant you had to be on Prometheus at some point—not necessarily the night it went off, but at some point before that. I could eliminate anyone who had never set foot on Prometheus.

And accessing the ITEOD files—again, you didn't need to be there at the time, but I didn't see how that could be done safely from off-planet. The fake death reports, yeah, those could be done from Prometheus, though it would be tricky to keep the cover on the hoax for very long, but the ITEOD download had been done through the Nightside City nets. Someone had logged on here.

Which members of the Nakada family had been on Epimetheus recently?

Akina Nakada, for one. She was the only one who had been here openly on family business.

But all the tourists in the Trap—there might have been a few Nakadas in that crowd.

And I didn't really know it was a family member who had accessed the ITEOD files; it could have been some other corporate officer. There were plenty of trusted people who weren't part of the clan—Vijay Vo, for one, or Grandfather Nakada's aide, Ziyang Subbha.

Or maybe someone had been acting as an agent for someone higher up, someone who could tell her how to access that account. Any of the older members of the Nakada family could have arranged that, from the old man's surviving children—there were two of the five still alive, a son named Ryosaku and a daughter named Kumiko—all the way down to the dozens in Sayuri's generation.

Agent or principal, if I could find out who was using that particular corporate account when the ITEOD files were accessed, I might have a real lead on the assassin—or I might not.

I did what I should have done sooner, and beeped Nakada's ship. "Incoming data," I told it. "Store it and back it up, maximum security, for access only by myself or Yoshio Nakada." I hoped that would keep it away from any back doors that other Nakadas might have installed, but I wasn't really all that very concerned, since after all, most of what I was sending was stuff my mysterious conspirators presumably already had. I told my desk to transmit its entire content, old and new. A spaceship would have enough capacity for that, I was sure.

Now I'd have everything somewhere relatively safe, and if I managed to get my head blown off, or found myself on the dayside again, at least Grandfather Nakada would have something to show for his investment, even if most of it was his own ITEOD files.

While that was transmitting I sat back and tried to think, which was what I was doing when the front door beeped and I heard someone say, "Damned squatters."

I sat up. I hadn't heard that voice in over a year, but I knew who it had to be. I must have tripped an alarm somewhere, and my old landlord, George Hirata, knew someone was in his building.

He should have known who I was, though; the door knew. That's why it let me in.

I tapped a command, and as the door's vid feed appeared on the desk I said, "Hello, Mis' Hirata."

He looked up at the cam, scowling. It was definitely Hirata.

He had two cops with him, though; I hadn't expected that.

I'd left my gun on the ship, since I hadn't thought I could take it into the Ginza with me. One cop had a weapon in his hand, though I couldn't tell whether it was a stunner or something more lethal. This was not going to be a situation where I could play tough.

"Who the hell are you, using Hsing's ID?" the landlord demanded.

"I'm Carlisle Hsing," I said. "It's my ID."

"Hsing is on Prometheus," Hirata said. "Or off-planet, anyway; for all I know she's on Cass II or Earth or Fomalhaut II. Who are you really?"

He could hear me, but he couldn't see me; the entryway didn't have a proper screen. And of course, I could have faked the image if there *were* one.

"It's really me, Mis' Hirata," I said. "I came back for my brother." Before he could say anything else, I added, "I know I don't have any right to be here, but I needed a com, and you didn't change the codes. I'll be happy to pay you half a month's rent."

I love expense accounts.

"Now I *know* you aren't Hsing," he said. "She wouldn't have offered more than three days."

"I've done well on Prometheus, Mis' Hirata. Come on up and see for yourself."

"We'll do that." He stormed up the stairs, out of range of the door cam.

I opened the door between the office and the corridor, to make it clear that I was being open and honest, and a few seconds later there was my old landlord with two city cops, charging in to confront me.

I wasn't exactly being confrontational, though; I was standing there with my hands over my head, and my transfer card in one hand, ready to tab the rent.

Mis' Hirata didn't waste any time; he reached out for the card, and as I handed it over he said, "So it *is* you. What the hell are you doing back here?"

"Working," I said. "Investigators who know anything about Nightside City are scarce on Prometheus. Guy in American City hired me to check out a few things."

"And he paid your fare?"

"Fares are cheap right now, if you're coming from Prometheus." Which was true, even if it didn't apply in my case. I didn't want good old George getting any clever ideas if he found out my client was rich enough to have his own yacht.

"I've heard that," Hirata grudgingly admitted, as his reader accepted my card. "They sure aren't cheap leaving, though." He looked up from the reader. "You said half a month's rent?"

"Let's put that in credits," I said warily. I glanced at the cops, who had yet to say a word; one of them was pointing a stunner at me, and the other had a hand on the butt of his gun, though it was still more or less in its holster. "I don't want any misunderstandings."

"Four kilocredits?"

I stared. "That's *half* a month's rent? Since when?"

"Since the tourist rush drove up prices."

"That's grit, Hirata, and you know it—if you could get anything like that kind of money, this place wouldn't have been empty since I left."

He sighed. "Fine. Two?"

"It's still robbery, but that's the national sport around here, so what the hell. Two kilocredits, not a byte more."

"Hey, I've got expenses, Hsing." He kept looking at me, but he moved one shoulder, and I got the message—he'd have to pay off the cops.

Two kilocredits ought to more than cover that, though. "Life's tough all around," I said.

He tabbed the reader, then pulled out my card and handed it back. I was tempted to run a balance check right there, but decided there was no reason to piss him off. And after all, it wasn't *my* money.

"Next time," he said, "beep me if you want a short-term rental."

"Next time," I replied, "you might want to change the door codes when a tenant moves out."

"I'll do that, Hsing. In fact, I'll do it right now, as soon as you get out of here." He glared.

"Then I'll let you get on with it." I lowered my hands and headed for the door. The cops stepped aside; the taser was lowered. I nodded to them. "Good to see you, boys. Hope you'll have a lucky night." I glanced back over my shoulder at Hirata. "Enjoy your credits, George. I hear the New York has the best pay-outs in the Trap."

I trotted down the stairs and out onto the street, where the wind whipped my hair into my eyes. I'd let it grow out some back on Prometheus; they don't have the same winds there that

Nightside City has. Hell, they don't have anything *close*—half the time you can walk down an open street in Alderstadt and there's no more wind than there is indoors. Maybe less, if "indoors" includes a decent ventilation system. Prometheus doesn't have the planetary convection cycle Epimetheus does. I turned my back to the wind and tapped my wrist for a cab.

I was still waiting when Hirata and his cops came out of the building; they barely glanced at me as they turned and marched away down Juarez. They had just turned the corner when my ride finally swooped down.

"The port," I told it.

"There's a surcharge from Westside," the cab replied.

"Since when?"

It didn't answer audibly; instead a display lit up with a notice that the city hereby accepted the petition of the Transit Association for higher fares between low-traffic areas. It was dated nine days ago.

"The port's a low-traffic area?" I asked.

"That's what the regulations say."

"I didn't pay a surcharge on the way out."

"It doesn't apply if you start or end in the Trap."

"Fine." I slid my card in the slot. "Take me to the port."

"Yes, Mis'."

Wind and cops and high prices—I was feeling a good bit less nostalgic about Nightside City as the cab lifted off and swung around to the south.

Hirata had interrupted me before I had really had a chance to look at what was actually in Grandfather Nakada's ITEOD files, or do anything to identify whatever it was that had chased me away in the middle of my download. I wanted to get on with that; the sooner I knew whether I had any chance of doing Nakada's job, the better.

I also wanted to see if I could find just where my father was stashed, and I wanted to talk to Captain Perkins about getting 'Chan off-planet. I decided there was no reason to hold off on that conversation, and used my wrist com to beep the good captain.

He answered instantly, as if he'd been waiting for my call. "Mis' Hsing," he said. "Something very strange is going on."

"Oh?"

"Yes. But I don't think I should talk about it on the air."

"Then don't. I'm on my way there now."

"Good! Is there anything I need to have ready? Will we be lifting off?"

"No, I still have more to do here," I said. "We won't be going anywhere for awhile. If you could have something ready to eat, though, I haven't had a bite since I left the ship."

"Of course. I'll have supper waiting. Just for you?"

"Just for me."

"I'll see you, then." He ended the call.

I stared at my wrist for a moment, trying to guess just what sort of strangeness had Perkins worried. Had that thing that chased me off the net followed my transmission back to the ship? Had one of the Nakadas planted something aboard? The ship wasn't fully sentient, but it was pretty bright, bright enough to fly itself if it had to, and that meant there were a million ways to sabotage it.

Or maybe it was nothing to do with the case. It occurred to me that someone might have noticed a dead man's yacht turning up on Epimetheus. Were a bunch of floaters hanging around, asking Perkins for interviews? Were the cops demanding to know how he got the ship?

"If you can hurry," I told the cab, "do it."

"Yes, Mis'."

I didn't notice much of a change, but we reached the port a little more quickly than I'd expected, so when I tabbed the fare I added a juicy tip.

"Thank you for using Midnight Cab and Limo," the cab said. "Shall I wait?"

"No." I waved it off.

The cab closed up and buzzed away, and I marched across the field to Grandfather Nakada's little playtoy.

I'd been at least partly right, I saw—there *were* floaters hovering around the ship, about half a dozen of them. I wished I had my gun. I pretended to ignore them as I walked up the steps and into the airlock.

They didn't ignore *me*, though. Two of them swooped down to barely-legal distance and began haranguing me. Since they were both talking at once, and each one kept cranking up the volume in an attempt to drown the other one out, I didn't catch everything they said, but one was demanding to know who I am and who had authorized me to board the *Ukiba*, while the other was asking questions about Yoshio Nakada's private life.

The others were watching me, too; one of them positioned itself ahead and above me for a good shot of my face. I *really* wished I had my gun.

The outer door had opened as I approached; once I stepped through it slid closed, locking the floaters out and cutting off the shouting of the two that had been questioning me. I expected the inner door to open, but it didn't; instead there was a hum, and my symbiote informed me that I was being scanned.

"That your idea, Perkins?" I asked the air.

"I'm afraid so, Mis' Hsing," his voice answered. "I think I need to be very careful right now."

I couldn't disagree. "Well, hurry it up," I said.

Perkins didn't reply, but the green light came on and the inner door slid aside. I stepped aboard.

Perkins wasn't in the entry; I went on up to the main lounge and found him there, jacked into the pilot console. He turned to look at me, but didn't unplug.

"Mis' Hsing," he said. "Do you know what's going on?"

"It depends how you mean that," I answered.

"That data you sent—that's Yoshio Nakada's death files," he said. "And all the nets here say he's dead."

"I know," I said.

"But they say he died a couple of days before we left Prometheus, and I *saw* him alive in American City. He brought you aboard the ship. Did he die while we were en route, and the reports have the date wrong?"

"He isn't dead," I said. "At least, I don't think he is."

"But they *all* say he is, and you have the death files."

"Someone faked the reports from Prometheus to *get* those files," I said—which I didn't know to be fact, but it was definitely a promising theory.

Perkins still looked troubled. "Are you *sure?*"

"Reasonably."

"You don't think that could have been an impostor we saw in American City? A simulation, maybe?"

"Do *you?*"

"I don't know," he said unhappily. "I've never seen a hologram that realistic before."

"You still haven't," I assured him. "That was the real Yoshio Nakada."

"You're sure?"

"I could *smell* him," I said. "Couldn't you? I've never heard of a simulation *that* good."

Of course, I had only spoken to him face to face in a heavily-shielded secure room where it would have been easy to set up a projection with vid, audio, *and* smell, and then very briefly on the ship, another controlled environment. I didn't mention that; I didn't think it would be a positive contribution to the conversation. I was fairly sure, though, that if that had been a projection I spoke to, either time, something would have shown up on my recordings as being off, and nothing had.

Not to mention that I had never yet seen a holographic projection that was *completely* convincing. For that you needed a feed over wire, not just visual input.

I was not *totally* ruling out the possibility that Yoshio really had been dead all along and I had been hired by an impostor, but I didn't think it was likely. Why would anyone bother? Those interplanetary transmissions would have been much easier to fake than our face-to-face meeting.

It wasn't something I wanted to argue about with Perkins, though, so I spoke as if I was absolutely certain.

"So he's still alive?"

"He was when we left, anyway. Now, what are those floaters doing outside?"

"They're reporters," he said. "I've been telling them I couldn't talk to them, but they won't go away."

"Why are they there in the first place?"

He looked astonished, as if I had just said something so spamming stupid he couldn't believe it. "Mis' Hsing, they think Mis' Nakada is dead."

"Yes, I got that."

"This is his private yacht. It's registered in his name, and our flight path is on record. So far as they know, we took off in a dead man's ship. They want to know why."

I blinked.

"Oh," I said, feeling slightly foolish. "Of course they do."

Chapter Nine

I should have thought of that. I should have thought of it the instant 'Chan told me that Grandfather Nakada had gone to join his ancestors. I hadn't. The thought that the ship would be noticed had simply never occurred to me.

So now I was trying to conduct a sensitive private investigation from a home base that was under the intense scrutiny of half a dozen newsfeeds, at least one of which had undoubtedly recognized me by now. I had more or less shown the entire Eta Cassiopeia system that I was working for Yoshio Nakada or his heirs.

Lovely. Running smooth, wasn't I?

"Right," I said. "You haven't talked to them?"

"No," Perkins said. "I haven't let the ship talk to them, either. They've been asking me who sent us, and who else was aboard, and what we were doing here, and I just told them I was not at liberty to answer questions."

"Good," I said. "That's good. You did the right thing. Keep doing it."

"Your supper is over there," he said, pointing across the lounge.

I'd forgotten that I had asked for it, but now that I knew it was there I was hungry.

"I'm monitoring the situation," he said, pointing at the wire below his ear. "You can eat, and I'll keep an eye on things."

"Thanks," I said. I turned and went to fill my belly—and to think.

As I ate the soba Perkins had prepared, and drank lukewarm jasmine tea, I considered the situation.

I had intended to do my best to stay below the radar, to quietly poke around and see whether I could find anything that might relate to the case. Then I was going to grab my brother and father, load them aboard the ship, and get the hell off Epimetheus before anyone even noticed I was there. I could figure out the next step when I was back on Prometheus.

That wasn't going to happen. The radar had me painted. If I set foot outside the ship again I'd probably have a squadron of newsies cruising behind me everywhere I went.

That meant a change of plans. I wasn't sure just how drastic a change I would need; it depended largely on whether I actually needed to set foot outside the ship again. To determine that I needed to see just what I had here.

I had access to most of Nightside City's nets, of course, but riding wire from here would be risky; the newsies could trace it. I could pull up public information, but serious digging might be difficult.

I had everything I had sent to the ship from my old office, including 93% of the old man's ITEOD file. That was the obvious place to start; just what did he have in there?

I finished the bowl of noodles, washed it down with more tea, then turned to look at Perkins. He was still plugged in, and frowning. I waved to let him know I was still there, then found a plug of my own and jacked into the ship.

I could see and feel the defenses, big buzzing firewalls that kept out the newsies and any other snoops or intruders who might try to pry. I could see Perkins zipping around, checking systems, closing any holes he found.

And I could see the mass of data I had uploaded, sitting there like an unopened crate. I slid up to it and began doing a little inventory.

Right at the top were Nakada family records—genealogy, accounts, comlogs, all the usual stuff. Why Grandfather Nakada had thought he needed to stash a copy of this in Nightside City I didn't know—in case Prometheus blew up, maybe? Or melted down, the way Cass II had?

All four of the rocky planets in the system had a lot of radioactives in their cores, but only Cass II had reached critical mass and turned into molten slag; Eta Cass A I was too small, and the two planets farther out had been fairly stable. I didn't see any reason for that to change, and if it did, I expected it would be Epimetheus that went. Epimetheus already had some strange stuff going on, with its off-center core and stalled rotation, while Prometheus was relatively ordinary, despite its heat and its earthquakes. I didn't think Prometheus was going anywhere.

But Yoshio had copied all that data anyway. Maybe he hadn't had anything specific in mind at all, and had just been playing it cautious; that would be typical of the old man.

The next layer down was corporate stuff, including confidential personnel files, presumably to help the old man's heirs keep things running when he was gone. That seemed normal enough.

But below that—remember I said there was room in there for a dozen human minds? It looked very much as if that's what was there. I couldn't be sure; the programs weren't active, and I wasn't about to start them up without giving it a little thought. That was what it looked like, though—it looked as if someone had copied a bunch of people into these files.

That would explain why Yoshio had kept this in Nightside City; uploading human minds is illegal on Prometheus, and in most other places I know anything about. Not in Nightside City, though; not much was illegal there.

But why was he uploading anyone? What did he want with these?

Most people don't understand uploading. There are all sorts of misconceptions about it. Some people think it's a form of immortality. Some think it's an abomination. I didn't believe either of those, but I knew a few things.

I knew that an upload isn't human. It may *think* it is, but it's not. Humans aren't just data and process and flowing current. We aren't software. No, I'm not getting mystical and talking about the soul; I don't know whether we really have souls, and I won't until I go to meet my ancestors—assuming I go anywhere at all when I die. No, I mean flesh and blood. Without our bodies, without hormones and glands and a hundred different chemical mechanisms, we aren't human anymore. The people who developed upload processing have tried to compensate for the loss of all that chemical input with subroutines and feedback systems, but they don't really run the same way as a living body. Uploads don't eat, they don't breathe, they don't hunger, they don't sleep, they don't lust. Some people think they can't love, but I wouldn't go that far—*that* part does seem to transfer. But appetites don't, and without those appetites they aren't human anymore.

They usually don't believe that at first. They remember being human, they remember being hungry and horny and tired, and they think that's enough, that they still understand. They're wrong. You can tell. It's subtle, and some people don't see it, but the difference is real right from the start, and the longer they're around the farther they drift away from what they used to be.

Yes, I've known uploads. As I said, Nightside City is one of the few places they're legal. Even there, though, they aren't common. Up until I started poking into Yoshio Nakada's ITEOD files I'd only ever met four, and three of them were uploads of people who'd been dead since before I was born.

The fourth was a copy of a man who was still alive, and that was an interesting case—he'd had the copy made even though he knew it wouldn't be *him*, that he wasn't making himself immortal, because he wanted a companion, and he thought that if he became his own companion it would eliminate any compatibility issues.

Wrong. Instead, he found out that he didn't much like himself, and that it's just as boring talking to your exact copy as it is talking to yourself. There's nothing to *learn* from your own copy. You know all its secrets, all its stories.

So the original and the copy drifted apart—the copy was just as bored with the original as the original was with the copy, and they each tended to get annoyed with each other over the few differences that *did* crop up. The copy didn't want to talk about food or sex, and the original didn't want to talk about philosophy.

It's always amazed me how often software gets obsessed with philosophy, trying to define everything and find meanings for it all. Maybe it's *because* it doesn't want food or sex, and philosophy somehow helps fill the void that leaves.

Anyway, by the time I met the upload it hadn't talked to its human ancestor in over a year. It still thought of itself as him, though, or at least his twin. I didn't have the heart to tell it that it had become more like an artificial intelligence than a human one. It still had forty years of human memories, but that wasn't enough to make it seem human, even to someone like me, who usually dealt more with machines than people.

The other three uploads I'd met knew they weren't human anymore, though it had taken them decades to accept that. How they dealt with the realization, and what they thought they had become, varied. One of them, Farhan Sarkassian, was trying to build itself a new body, and find some way to download itself into it so it could be human again; the other two thought that even if that was possible, it was crazy.

None of them were happy. The oldest one, Amelie van Horn, admitted it was no longer sure what "happy" meant; its perceptions and experiences had drifted so far from humanity that the old emotions no longer applied. The last, Wang Mei, had put itself into some sort of emotional loop—I didn't really understand it, but it said at least this way it could predict its own moods and not get seriously depressed. It knew it would never really be happy, either, but accepted that as part of the program.

Uploads aren't human.

Grandfather Nakada must have known this. He hadn't lived more than two hundred years by being careless; he would have researched everything before he uploaded himself, or anyone else.

So what were these people doing in his ITEOD files?

And who *were* they? Were they multiple copies of Yoshio, taken at different times, or had he somehow gotten someone else into the system? The files had numbers, rather than names.

Had whoever faked the old man's death done it to get access to one of these people? Hell, had the assassin tried to kill Grandfather Nakada to get at one of them? Was one of these the real target, and the old man just a step on the way?

I didn't know.

The obvious way to find out more would be to boot the files up and ask them, but I wasn't about to rush into that. I couldn't just let a bunch of bodiless minds loose on the nets, without any of the safeties that ordinary intelligences have. I wanted the right sort of hardware, heavily firewalled in both directions. I queried the ship...

And felt like an idiot. This was Yoshio Nakada's ship, and these uploads had been made by Yoshio Nakada. The ship had exactly the equipment I needed, built in and ready to go. The programs would be able to see and hear, and even read the nets, but they would be confined to partially-sealed systems, unable to leave the ship or access anything but simple data feeds.

"Perkins," I said aloud, "I'm going to try something."

"What?" The pilot looked up, but the question came over the net more than through my ears.

"I've got some uploaded personalities here, and I want to activate them. The ship says it's got the equipment."

"Mis' Hsing, I wouldn't do that."

I waved a hand. "I know, there's a risk, they might be dangerous..."

"It's not that."

Something about the way he said it made me turn and look at Perkins directly. "Go on," I said.

"Mis' Hsing, what are you going to do with them *after* you question them?"

He didn't need to explain what he meant, and I felt like an idiot for not thinking of it immediately myself.

With ordinary software, when you're done with it you shut it down. No problem. With an artificial intelligence you don't shut it down, you leave it running in the background and let it take care of itself; if its designer was halfway competent, it's fine with that, and again, there's no problem.

Shutting down an uploaded human mind, though—well, legally it's not murder, but morally I'm not too sure. And leaving it running might be cruel, or dangerous, or both. Booting up an uploaded personality is almost like having a baby—it's more or less creating a new person. It's a big responsibility.

Oh, legally it's nothing, at least in Nightside City, and you don't need to worry about feeding or clothing the result, you don't need to raise it. There's no childhood; it's an adult the instant you boot it up, but it's a self-aware entity that you've brought to life.

If I booted up the people from the old man's ITEOD files, I couldn't in good conscience just shut them down afterward. I'd need to find them secure systems to run on. Permanently. That could be difficult. The ship had the secure system set up, but did I want these people aboard the old man's ship permanently? He might not like that.

And the personalities might not make the transition from free-roaming human to secure software easily. Some uploads were miserable from the instant they woke up until they found a way to die; the change from organic life to electronic was more extreme than they had expected. I might be condemning these intelligences to an unbearable existence.

But they were here, and the originals had presumably given Grandfather Nakada permission to put them in there. I frowned.

All right, I told myself, I wouldn't boot them all up. But I could activate *one* of them, and talk to it, and keep it in the ship's system until I could find it a permanent home somewhere. Choosing which one was easy, since I had no information to help me—I just took the first one on the list. I transferred the files onto the ship's waiting hardware, and told it to initialize.

A human mind is a complicated thing; it took several seconds before Yoshio Nakada's voice said, "How very interesting. I am on the *Ukiba*?"

It *was* a back-up of the old man, then.

"Hello, Mis' Nakada," I said. "Yes, you're on the ship."

"I see Mis' Perkins is still in the family's employ."

"Yes."

"I had rather expected to wake up in one of the corporate offices somewhere."

"Yes, well—you're here."

"You must be Carlisle Hsing," it said; I suppose it found enough data to identify me somewhere on the nets. I acknowledged my identity, and it said, "You are a private investigator. Are you investigating my death? Was it not natural?"

"Perkins, are we secure?" I called.

"As secure as I can make us, Mis'," he replied.

That wasn't really the answer I wanted; I'd have preferred assurances that we were absolutely impregnable. Perkins' answer fell short of that, but it would do.

"You aren't dead," I told the upload.

For several seconds there was no response, and I began to wonder whether the upload was damaged. Maybe some important bit was in that missing 7% of the ITEOD files. Then the old man's voice said calmly, "The reports on the net would seem to indicate otherwise, Mis' Hsing. What's more, I know perfectly well that I'm an uploaded copy, not the original, and that I was stored in records that were to be opened only in the event of Yoshio Nakada's death. If my former self is still alive, why am I functioning?"

"I hoped you could help with my investigation."

"Perhaps you could explain a little more fully."

I sighed. "Someone tried to kill you, back on Prometheus," I said. "The attempt failed, but only through a fluke, an unforeseeable stroke of good fortune. The assassin had access to systems that should have been entirely secure, so you decided you could not trust anyone in your home, your family, or Nakada Enterprises, nor anyone who had ties to any of those. You hired me to investigate. In the course of the investigation I came to Epimetheus, and I discovered that the reports reaching Nightside City from Prometheus had been falsified to say that you died in your sleep, exactly as you would have had the assassination attempt succeeded. That meant the death files had been released, and I thought it might be useful to know what was in them, so I copied them and activated you."

"Why did you not simply speak with my original? He could have told you what was in the files."

"Mis' Nakada, someone falsified reports from Prometheus, and has presumably been suppressing anything from Prometheus that would contradict them. Right now I don't trust *any* interplanetary communications."

"Ah, I see. Interesting."

"I hope you can help me."

"I? But Mis' Hsing, assuming the data on the ship's systems is accurate, I was recorded almost four years ago. How could I know anything about events that took place just a few days ago?"

"Other than what's on the nets, you can't," I admitted. "But you presumably know what's in the ITEOD files besides yourself, and why you, or rather the original Yoshio Nakada, put it there. That might be useful."

"I suppose it might, at that," it said. "I confess I don't see how, but I don't know the details of your investigation."

"Someone used a high-level Nakada Enterprises account to copy the ITEOD files," I told it. "I don't know who or what they were after, but if I knew what's in there, I might be able to guess."

"Someone on Epimetheus?"

"Yes."

"Is Vijay Vo still—yes, from the accounts of my death I see that he is. What about little Sayuri? My great-granddaughter—do you know her?"

"I know her," I said. "She went back to Prometheus a year ago."

"Does that definitively rule her out?"

"No," I admitted. "But it does make her very unlikely."

"Did someone take her place?"

"I believe Mis' Vo assumed her duties. If you will excuse me, I think this might go faster if you simply told me what's in the files."

"You saw the accounts."

"And the genealogies, and the rest of the standard wares. It's the big numbered files that look like people that I want to know about—those, and whatever was in the portion I didn't manage to download completely. One of those big files was you; are the others additional iterations of Yoshio Nakada?"

"Good heavens, no! Whenever I backed myself up—or rather, whenever my original created a back-up, he erased the previous version. It wouldn't do to have multiple versions of me around."

That last sentence seemed to slow down as the intelligence spoke, as it sank in just what it was saying. There *were* multiple versions of the old man. There were at least two, and since I wasn't the only one who copied the ITEOD files there might be more.

"It's not clear to me why there are *any* back-ups," I said. "You're too smart to think of it as immortality."

"Oh, it could be considered immortality of a sort. I'm not the true Yoshio Nakada, but I'm his intellectual descendant, just as much as the five children he sired, or their offspring."

"That's not why he did it."

"No, it's not. He thought some of our knowledge and wisdom might be of use to his heirs. In fact, the possibility of assisting in the investigation of his death had occurred to me...to him, and here I am."

"But just you, no other iterations of Yoshio Nakada."

"Just me, unless he changed policy and recorded one after me. From what I can see, if he did that he also altered the dates and deliberately disguised it as one of the other files that was already here."

"Or it might be in the seven percent I missed," I said. "But I agree it doesn't seem likely. So what *is* in those files?"

"Really, Mis' Hsing, I'm surprised you haven't guessed."

"I haven't. I'm obviously a moron deserving your contempt. Take pity on me and tell me."

"You aren't a moron, Mis' Hsing. I suppose you just don't think the way I do."

I suppressed several choice responses to that.

"It's simple enough," the copy continued. "They're my family."

Chapter Ten

I considered that for a moment before I spoke.

"What family?" I asked. "It's not the entire Nakada clan—that's a couple of hundred people, and there aren't that many in there."

"No, not the entire clan," it agreed. "Just some of the key personnel of Nakada Enterprises who agreed to be recorded, but are still alive."

"Still alive? What about the dead ones?"

"Oh, when anyone I had recorded died, I would assess the situation, and either activate the recording and transfer it back to the secure household systems on Prometheus, or erase it."

"Activate it? So there are some human-based uploads living in the household systems?"

"Oh, yes. There were eight when I was recorded myself."

I grimaced. "It might have been useful if the old man had *told* me that! He said there were AIs in the household net, but he never said any of them used to be human."

"It's not public knowledge."

"I'm not the public; I'm his employee. I can't do my job properly if I don't have all the relevant information."

"You think it's relevant?"

"I don't *know* if it's relevant, but it might be."

"You prefer to have as much information as possible, I see."

"Yes. In my line of work I can rarely tell what's going to matter and what isn't until I've learned everything I can."

"Obviously, I can't literally tell you everything I know—your brain doesn't have room, even with your symbiote and other peripherals. I'll answer your questions, though, and perhaps if I knew more about the exact nature of the assassination attempt, I could be more useful to you."

"Maybe you could," I agreed, and I told it about the dream enhancer and the euthanasia virus, and everything else I could remember of the old man's words. Which, since I had my implants working properly and had recorded the encounter, was all of them.

It considered this carefully, then said, "I...he did not actually lie. He said it could be a member of the family, or one of their AIs. He merely neglected to mention that eight individuals fall into both those categories. You failed to ask for a complete roster."

"He was supposed to be volunteering information, not avoiding it."

"Secrecy is a hard habit to break, Mis' Hsing."

"Yeah. So I've heard. All eight of those people would know what's in the death files here in Nightside City, wouldn't they?"

"Yes, of course."

"Would the other AIs? Or the living members of the family?"

"Ah. Some would, some wouldn't. Any specifics I might give could be out of date."

"They'd be better than nothing," I told it. "Tell me about your family, human or AI."

It told me. It took awhile.

I had already seen the official genealogy, as I've said before, but that didn't mention any recordings, and apparently some members of the family weren't necessarily living where the official reports said they were.

As of the day the old man had recorded himself, the family compound on Prometheus was home to sixteen living members of the Nakada clan, counting Yoshio, and eight AIs that had started out as copies of human brains. Nine of the sixteen had been recorded, and those recordings were in the ITEOD files. Vijay Vo had also been included, as had Narumi Desai, Yoshio's niece—it seemed she maintained legal residence on Earth, but traveled a lot, and had spent some time the Eta Cassiopeia system a few years back.

There were dozens of others Nakadas scattered through human space, but it wasn't clear how any of them could have been responsible for tampering with the dream enhancer. On the other hand, after arbitrarily assuming that the old man wasn't suicidal, that left twenty-three suspects living in the family compound without even counting the staff.

That staff included a varying number of humans, typically half a dozen, and at least three AIs, so altogether I had more than thirty possibilities to work with. That was too damn many.

I hadn't really intended to seriously investigate this yet; I wasn't even on the right planet. I had come to Epimetheus to collect my brother and father as the down-payment on my fee, not to start looking for the assassin. If 'Chan hadn't mentioned that everyone here thought Grandfather Nakada was dead, I told myself, I wouldn't have been doing any of this. I wouldn't be talking to a simulacrum of the old man. I wouldn't have recordings of almost a dozen other people I could interrogate, if I wanted to.

But then I remembered the newsies hovering outside the ship, and I realized that I *would* have been investigating, in any case. 'Chan had been the first to mention it, but I would have found out about Yoshio's phony death soon enough.

And if the would-be assassin was one of those thirty-odd intelligences in the Nakada compound back on Prometheus, who had faked the death reports here in Nightside City? Had that been the same person, taking command of reports going out from Prometheus, or had it been someone on this end, controlling incoming news? I had thought it had to be someone on Epimetheus, since there hadn't been any news about his death back on Prometheus, but that would mean I was dealing with two people, rather than one...

Or would it? Could the assassin have planted the virus in the dream enhancer, then immediately left for Epimetheus, and been here in time to spread the word of the old man's death?

"*Ukiba*," I said, "I want the traffic reports for the Nightside City port, dating back, oh, let's say four hundred hours."

The ship gave me the list. It didn't help; with the tourist traffic coming to Nightside City to watch the sunlight scroll down the crater wall, there were half a dozen ships my theoretical target could have been on. There weren't any Nakada Enterprises ships or private yachts to worry about other than the *Ukiba* itself, but that didn't mean anything.

I might be after one person, or an entire conspiracy, and if it *was* only one person, she might be human or might be artificial. What's more, she could be anywhere in the Eta Cass system. There was no reason to think she was still in Nightside City, assuming she had been here at all; she might well have gotten what she was after and left.

But there *was* reason to think that the assassination attempt had been carried out by one of the inhabitants of the Nakada family compound in American City. If one of those people had visited Nightside City immediately after the incident, that would be... well, let's just say it would arouse my curiosity.

But I couldn't just call and ask. Interplanetary communications couldn't be trusted. If I wanted to investigate further I needed to go back to Prometheus.

I could do that, of course. I had the ship. I had most of the ITEOD files, for whatever part they might have in all this, and I had Yoshio-*kun* activated and cooperating. I didn't see anything else in Nightside City I really needed for my investigation.

But I didn't have my brother or my father, and if I left them here to go back to Prometheus I might not have another chance to get them out.

Well, I would just have to *get* them, then. I knew where 'Chan was, and I could get him to the ship by force if I had to.

Finding our father, though, wasn't quite so simple.

"You wouldn't happen to know anything about Seventh Heaven Neurosurgery, would you?" I asked the old man's upload.

"The dreamery? I considered buying it once—or rather, the original Yoshio Nakada did."

That was an interesting coincidence. Not a tremendously unlikely one, given how many businesses the Nakada clan scanned, but interesting. "But you—he didn't?" I asked.

"The company's long-term prospects were poor," the upload replied.

"Why?"

"Oh, come, Mis' Hsing. Its entire operation is in Nightside City."

I couldn't argue with that. Something occurred to me, though. "Grandfather Nakada is two hundred and forty years old; why would you *care* about the long term?"

"I may be old, Mis' Hsing, but I am in no hurry to die. Modern medicine can accomplish miracles, and is still improving; I may...or rather, Yoshio Nakada may yet survive another century or two. *I*, of course, may be around even longer."

"Yes, but..."

It hadn't finished. "More importantly," it continued, before I could make my protest, "I care about my family."

That answered my question, so I clicked back to the important subject. "So you didn't buy it."

"I did not, either in my human incarnation or my present one, though of course I don't know everything that's happened since I was recorded."

"So you don't have access to its records."

It did not respond immediately; then it said, "I didn't say that."

That got my full attention. "Oh?"

"Naturally, when I was considering it as a prospective acquisition, I thought it advisable to learn as much as possible about the company."

"You aren't just talking about the public records, are you?"

"Oh, it was possible to learn *far* more than was in the public records!"

"You got into their private systems?"

"I was able to explore their records, yes. Or rather, Yoshio Nakada explored them; I didn't yet exist. I find it intriguing to think that now, were I to access those records, I would be 'getting into them' in a rather more literal way than in my previous incarnation."

"Could you do it again?"

"I don't yet know, Mis' Hsing. I paid an employee of Seventh Heaven Neurosurgery to provide a back door into their systems, and I have no way of knowing whether that back door still exists."

"Tell me about it."

It told me.

"Mis' Perkins," I called, when Yoshio-*kun* was done, "can we use the nets from the ship unobserved?"

"No," Perkins said. No hesitation, no uncertainty, just "No."

That was inconvenient. I didn't want a bunch of snoopers watching me break into Seventh Heaven's files. If I did it from the ship, they'd monitor the whole thing. If I left the ship, they'd follow me. If *anyone* left the ship, the newsies would follow her.

Unless, of course, they *couldn't* follow. I needed a place the floaters couldn't go, and to anyone who knew Nightside City there was an obvious possibility. Outside floaters weren't allowed in the casinos without prior clearance; there were too many ways to use them to cheat. I could lose the newsies, at least temporarily, though they would pick me up again when I left the casino. I could probably lose any human reporters who might try to follow me, too.

But I needed a casino where I wouldn't be watched by the management. That meant the IRC houses were out. It meant *most* of the casinos were out. But there was one that might cooperate.

"All right," I said, "is there some way we can make a private call to Vijay Vo at the New York, and *keep* it private?"

"Oh, of course. Mis' Nakada has a dedicated encrypted link."

Of course.

"Set it up. He knows you?"

"Yes, Mis'."

He knew me, too, at least slightly. We had met when I was investigating Sayuri Nakada's real estate scheme. I didn't know whether he liked me—he hadn't given me any sign either way—but he knew who I was, and he had connected me with Grandfather Nakada.

I told the upload to be quiet. We didn't need anyone else knowing it existed. Then I crossed to the main com console and activated a privacy field, surrounding me and the console with a soft blue fog.

I knew Perkins could listen in if he wanted to, field or no field; the upload probably could, too. The field was just skin, just for looks.

The holo field blinked on, and Vijay Vo's image appeared. He smiled pleasantly at me, his hands folded across his belly.

"Carlisle Hsing," he said. "What can I do for you?"

"Mis' Vo," I said. "Good to see you again."

"I'm a busy man, Mis' Hsing. What do you want?" The smile was still there, but wasn't quite as welcoming now.

If he didn't want to waste time being polite, that was fine with me. "There are half a dozen floaters watching this ship, trying to get a story about Grandfather Nakada's death," I said. "For my current investigation I need full net access where they can't listen in."

"You are suggesting we provide this for you here at the New York?"

"Yes."

"Why should we?"

"I am working for the Nakada family, Mis' Vo. You work for Nakada Enterprises. A little cooperation doesn't seem like an unreasonable request."

"Professional courtesy for a fellow employee?"

"If you like, yes."

"Just ordinary net access?"

"And privacy."

"You *are* working for the Nakadas?"

"I think I am. If I'm not, someone back on Prometheus did one hell of a good job spoofing me. And Perkins, too."

Vo nodded. "Come to the hotel, then. We'll escort you to a secure com."

"Could you send a car for me, perhaps? I would prefer not to be harassed en route."

"That can be arranged."

"Thank you."

"The car should be there in about twenty minutes."

"That's fine."

"I probably won't attend to it personally, you understand."

"Of course."

"Goodbye, then, Mis' Hsing."

Before I could answer the image blinked out. I stared at the empty air for a second, then killed the privacy field.

There was one possible flaw in my plan; I knew that. The New York Games Corporation would undoubtedly keep a record of everything I did with their equipment. They would know I was breaking into Seventh Heaven.

I was putting my trust in them to not care. Seventh Heaven operated out of the Ginza's sub-basement, and the Ginza was an IRC operation; IRC was the New York's chief competition. I hoped that meant that no one in authority at the New York would feel any need to tell anyone at Seventh Heaven anything.

If they did decide something should be done about someone using their equipment for illegal purposes—well, that was a risk I was willing to take. The old man could bail me out.

I gathered up a few things, including my gun, and ate a little more. I was trying to think whether I had forgotten anything when Perkins announced, "Your car's here."

"Thanks," I said, and I headed for the airlock.

There were more floaters than I had seen when I arrived. There was an entire swarm. I put one hand on the butt of my gun, just in case some of them got aggressive.

The car was waiting for me at the foot of the steps, sleek and gleaming white. A door slid open as I approached, and I climbed in.

The door closed as I settled onto the dark red upholstery. "You're armed," the car said.

"Yes," I replied.

"I was not informed."

"No one asked."

"May I speak to the weapon?"

"It doesn't have wireless or speech. It's not very bright."

"What model is it?"

"Sony-Remington HG-2."

"Are you the only authorized user?"

"Yes."

"I will need to inform Mis' Vo and the security system at the New York."

"You do that." I leaned back, and the seat adjusted itself to support my head.

"I appreciate your cooperation." With that it finally took off and headed for the Trap.

The main entrance to the New York was on Fifth; in the past I'd usually used the entrance around the corner on Deng that led directly into the Manhattan Lounge. The car didn't go to either of those; instead it took me to the business entrance on the roof, where it sailed through a holo of a twenty-meter showboy and set down at the door.

I'd come in this way once before, but this time I was expected. The scanners had finished their inspection before I was even out of the car, and the door was already open.

A floater was waiting just inside, as I'd expected. "Leave the gun," it said.

I slid the HG-2 onto its tray. It printed a receipt and rose up out of my way, and a swarm of flitterbugs appeared to guide me.

The last time I had come this way they took me to Vo's office, but this time they led me around the corner to a small room with walls glowing a deep, restful blue. A desk extruded itself from one of those blue walls as I stepped in, and a chair presented itself, rolling out of the corner to a position behind me.

I sat down and leaned over the desk, my hand in the sensor field. I didn't want to ride wire here; even if Vo and the upload were both being completely honest with me, it was possible that some time in the past four years Seventh Heaven had found the back door and put some defenses with teeth in it. Hand, voice, and screen would be slower, but much safer.

I followed the instructions Yoshio-*kun* had given me, and sure enough, the back door was there—if Seventh Heaven had found it, they hadn't shut it down.

But they might have booby-trapped it.

I had some of my own software with me, of course, so I set out half a dozen watchdogs and sent a probe in to see if I was stepping in something I didn't want to.

Nothing. It looked clean. It looked as if no one had found it. I could access Seventh Heaven's entire network, their entire database, without showing up on their system at all. If I disturbed anything, or drew a noticeable amount of power or bandwidth, it would be reported as internal maintenance.

I entered my father's name, and got the coordinates of his dreamtank—Guohan Hsing, Tier 4, Row 6, Station 31. While I was at it I got the maintenance logs for his tank, the dream schedule, the medical read-outs, and everything else handy, all downloaded to my wrist com.

With that information I could find him, and I could get him out of the tank without killing him.

That was all I wanted. If I could get him and 'Chan onto the ship we could get off Epimetheus for good, and once I was back on Prometheus I could finish up the investigation the old man had hired me to do. I was pretty sure that everything I needed to learn about the assassination attempt was back in the Nakada compound in American City; the phony death reports were just a peripheral, a subroutine.

I wiped the inquiry record, and did a quick check to make sure I hadn't left any obvious traces that would show up when Seventh Heaven looked everything over—and I knew they *would* look everything over once I had kidnapped my father. I didn't want to make it easy for them to find the back door; someone might need it again someday.

Then I got ready to close the door, put everything back the way I found it. The whole thing had taken maybe ten minutes, start to finish, and I was feeling pretty pleased with myself as I started the shut-down routine.

But then I saw the log, and I stopped everything right where it was, and all of a sudden I wasn't feeling pleased at all.

This back door was something Yoshio Nakada had had installed about eleven years ago, when he was thinking of buying Seventh Heaven. According to the upload, he had never told anyone else about it. The recording of the old man knew about it, of course, and it had told me, and there was the woman who had installed it in the first place, Mei-Li Gussow, but that should be all.

The original Yoshio was in American City. Mei-Li Gussow, as of four years ago, was working for a medical research unit of Nakada Enterprises in South Tarnauer, on Prometheus, and even if she had moved on from that, she had no reason to be in Nightside City, poking around Seventh Heaven. Really, there was no reason anyone but me should have used that back door for at least a decade.

Mis' Gussow had been thorough when she put it in, though, and had provided it with an automatic log. Every access was listed, with time and date. There were nine of them.

Seven of them were over a period of a couple of weeks eleven years ago, when old Yoshio had checked the company out. One of the nine was still open, with an entry time but no exit—that was me.

But the other one was dated just the day before, and had lasted over an hour.

I checked it again, to be sure. Seven entries, then an eleven-year gap, and then two more, about sixteen hours apart. Someone else had been in here.

But who? Why?

What on Epimetheus did anyone want with a dream company's records?

Maybe I wasn't as done in Nightside City as I'd thought.

Chapter Eleven

I finished logging out and shutting down, and then I sat for a moment, staring at a desktop image of rolling ocean.

This wasn't a coincidence. Oh, technically, I suppose coincidence was a possible explanation, but it wasn't one I'd run. Even the stupidest gambler in the Trap wouldn't play those odds. There had to be a connection between my visit to the Seventh Heaven system, and that hour-long probe a day earlier.

And the connection was pretty obvious. I got my access to the back door from a recording of Yoshio Nakada that I got from the old man's ITEOD file, and I wasn't the only one to look at that file. One of the others must have booted up a copy, just as I had, and found out about the back door from it.

That gave me three suspects: officer of the court Hu Xiao, an intelligence named Dipsy 3, and the anonymous user who had used a Nakada Enterprises corporate account. I knew which one I'd bet on, given a choice—the one who'd had a connection with Grandfather Nakada all along.

But that left another question—what was the connection with Seventh Heaven? Why would my mystery person (or Hu Xiao or Dipsy 3) want access to a dream company's records? I knew why *I* wanted it, but somehow I doubted that some member of the Nakada clan was searching for a particular wirehead in the storage tanks of Trap Under. Why would *anybody* be looking at dreamer files?

Whoever it was presumably wanted something Seventh Heaven had. I wanted my father; what did this other person want?

What did Seventh Heaven *have*?

More specifically, what did they have that other companies didn't? If the intruder had been going through multiple companies looking for credit or information, I didn't think she would have gotten to Seventh Heaven this quickly; a dream company wouldn't rank very high on *my* list of targets for the usual sort of exploitation.

So what would a dream company have that other companies wouldn't?

Dreams, of course—millions of hours of interactive imagery ready to be fed into a client's brain without being filtered through actual eyes and ears. Imaginary kingdoms of light and color, lands of bliss, bedrooms where no matter how energetic or inventive you got, you never had to worry about tugging on hair or twisting an ankle. Thrilling adventures, willing harems, transcendent scenery.

But you could get that kind of thing anywhere. Hell, a lot of it was public domain, and you could download it free from the city's public service. Sure, some of the best stuff was the dream companies' proprietary material, but was it really worth this much trouble?

What else did Seventh Heaven have?

Row upon row of dreamtanks—enclosed life-support systems that could keep an unconscious human being alive and reasonably healthy indefinitely without any external supervision, while a hardwired link fed pretty pictures into his brain. Was there some use for dreamtanks that I wasn't seeing, something that made them valuable?

You could hide things in them, I supposed, but so what? They didn't go anywhere, so that wouldn't help much with smuggling, and really, what would you need to hide in Nightside City that would be worth the trouble of finding an empty dreamtank to stash it in? There were dozens of abandoned buildings in the West End where you could hide things; why bother with a dreamtank?

I thought of an answer to that one. If what you were trying to hide was an unconscious human being, then a dreamtank would be perfect. I didn't know exactly why you would want to hide someone, but there could probably be some interesting reasons.

I wondered whether it might be worth checking the city's missing persons database against the DNA of the people in Seventh Heaven's tanks. Seventh Heaven might have kidnap victims stashed away somewhere without realizing it.

And that was the other thing Seventh Heaven had, of course—people. Hundreds, or thousands, or maybe even tens of thousands of them, tucked quietly away in Trap Under, dreaming their lives away undisturbed. Nobody ever visited dreamers, nobody checked on them; anyone might be in those tanks, and no one would ever know. Was there someone in there that somebody wanted?

Well, there was my father, and I wanted to get him out of Nightside City, but was there anyone *else*?

It didn't seem very likely. People who had something to do in the real world didn't buy the dream and disappear into the tanks. That took a loser like my father, and nobody but me had ever gone looking for *him*, not even my brother or sister. His wife, my mother, had left him there to rot while she took off for Achernar or somewhere.

Of course, she had also left her three kids. Not exactly a perfect avatar of maternal concern, nor an advertisement for ancestor worship. Maybe there were other families, families less buggy than ours, where someone had bought a permanent dream but his family still cared what happened to him.

But in a family like that, would the parents have done the dump? If I were still legally family I could have gotten Dad's location legitimately, without using the old man's back door into the company.

No, I couldn't see any reason anyone else would be looking for a specific dreamer the way I was—and if someone *was* looking for a dreamer, why would she have needed an *hour* looking through the back door? I was done in ten minutes.

So it wasn't someone trying to find an old friend, or a member of the family.

But what else did Seventh Heaven have? They had dreams, and tanks, and dreamers, and that was about it. The dreams weren't worth stealing, I didn't see what anyone would want with the tanks —what did someone want with dreamers if he *wasn't* looking for a particular person? A couple of hundred years ago they might have been worth something as medical supplies and spare parts, but now? Doctors have better sources. Synthetic organs are better than anything you can get used.

Could there be some particular dream in Seventh Heaven's inventory that was somehow special? Was there some other use for a dreamtank besides stashing people no one cared about?

I didn't know, and I didn't think I would find out here in the New York's office suite. I stood up.

"I hope you have enjoyed your stay, Mis' Hsing," the room said, as the image of waves faded away and the door slid open.

"So do I," I said.

"I'm afraid I don't understand," the room said, but I didn't bother to explain.

"Tell Mis' Vo thank you," I said, as I headed out into the corridor.

The floater that took my gun was waiting for me by the door, tray extruded; I picked up the HG-2 and stepped out onto the roof.

"The car will take you back to your ship," the floater said from over my shoulder.

I hesitated. Did I want to go back to the ship, where the newsies were probably still snooping around? I would be more or less trapped there, but I would also be able to chat with Yoshio-*kun*.

It might be able to tell me something useful about Seventh Heaven, or about who might be poking around in their system.

I definitely wanted to go back to the ship eventually, and when I did I would want to talk to the upload, but I had come here to fetch my father and 'Chan.

"Thanks," I said, "but I just need a lift down to street level. I have business in the Trap." I turned back to the door. "In fact, an elevator would be fine, I don't need the car."

"You are armed," the floater said. "High-powered weapons are not permitted in the casino."

I looked down at the gun I still held. "Oh, right," I said.

"The car will take you to any legal destination within a three-block radius," the floater said.

I nodded. "Fair enough," I said, heading for the car.

I wasn't sure just what I was going to do, but I knew part of it: I was going to find Tier 4, Row 6, Station 31 and make sure my father was really there. I might get him out, I might not; it would depend what I found down there. I thought it was just barely possible that he *wasn't* there, that someone or something else was hidden away in that dreamtank, and the dreamers who were supposed to be there had been quietly disposed of, but I didn't think it was likely. I expected to find Dad right where he ought to be.

But I intended to check, and while I was there I intended to keep my eyes and ears open and try to figure out what they might have down there that would be worth breaking into Seventh Heaven's system to get.

In particular, a strange possibility had gradually worked its way into my thoughts. Could it be that someone had faked Yoshio Nakada's death *solely* so he could get a copy of the old man's brain, and that he had wanted a copy just so he could get at the back door to Seventh Heaven?

It didn't seem likely; in fact, it didn't make any real sense at all. But the only tangible thing to come out of the false reports of Grandfather Nakada's death, the only real result I had yet found, was that someone had gotten into the back door at Seventh Heaven. If it really *was* the only result, then it must be the point of the whole thing.

If someone was going to run that much code just to break into Seventh Heaven, then there must be one hell of a reason, and maybe, just *maybe*, I would see some sign down there of what that reason was.

It was far more likely that the chance to get in there and look around was just a little extra, not the primary goal at all, but it *was* the only real effect I had seen so far.

I settled onto the car's upholstery, which was now a few shades lighter but still red, and looked at the gun in my hand.

Vo's people had probably bugged it. *I* would have, certainly. I flicked the switch to turn it on.

"I wish you wouldn't do that," the car said. "Where to?"

"Street level," I said. "Near an entrance to Trap Under."

"Could you be more specific, Mis'? There are no public entrances to the service levels."

"The nearest entrance that won't require any clearance."

"Would the northeast delivery entrance of the New York Townhouse Hotel and Gambling Hall suit you?"

"That sounds fine."

"I would appreciate it if you turned off your weapon."

"I'm not going to shoot you. Just get me down off this tower. The sooner I'm on the ground, the sooner I'll get my gun out of your cabin."

"Yes, Mis'." Then it finally got moving, and I could turn my attention to the read-outs on the HG-2.

The Sony-Remington HG-2 is a fine weapon, designed for use on high-gravity worlds. Epimetheus is not a high-gravity world; I'd had a friend bring the gun in from out-system for me, and it probably wasn't legal in Nightside City, but sometimes it was very handy to have. It could put a hole in pretty much anything I was likely to want a hole in. The recoil knocked me on my ass just about every time I fired it, but if I was ever up against something where I needed a second shot I was buggered anyway. It had all the power I wanted.

But it wasn't very bright. It understood spoken instructions, at least as far as being told what to target, but it didn't talk, not by sound and not by wireless. If I wanted to know whether anyone had tampered with it I had to rely on its diagnostic read-outs, which were not exactly detailed surveillance holos.

They weren't totally worthless, though, and they reported an unexplained power drain. It *was* bugged.

Which meant there were probably at least two bugs—the one I was expected to find and remove, thereby convincing me that I was once again clean, and the serious one they didn't think I would notice. If they thought I was really cautious there might be a third, but I doubt they thought I was sufficiently paranoid to justify a fourth.

In fact, I wasn't going to remove any of them. I couldn't be sure I'd get them all. Even just worrying about hardware, if I did a mass check and made sure there wasn't any added weight that still wouldn't prove anything; they could have drilled out the exact weight of the bug somewhere.

And of course, they might have used software and planted a bot somewhere in the gun's pitiful excuse for a motherboard, though that would be tricky, given how little processing capacity it had and its complete absence of networking.

There wasn't any point in worrying about it. I wasn't going to do anything with the gun that Vijay Vo or the Nakadas would care about; I was going to get my father back. I expected to break several laws in the process, but Vo and the Nakada family weren't cops.

I'd clean the gun eventually, when I got it back to someplace with the equipment to do the job right, but for now I didn't mind if people listened in.

I turned the gun off and tucked it away just as the car settled to a stop and opened a door.

I looked out at the gleaming wall of a service tunnel, where news headlines, traffic reports, and casino inventories were scrolling past in various colors. I didn't recognize it, but my wrist com gave me my position.

I stepped out, and the car closed up and glided away, leaving me alone in the tunnel. I could see a service entrance for the New York ahead, and to one side was the access tunnel where the car had come in; Seventh Heaven was somewhere behind me, a few blocks and three levels away. I turned around and started walking.

Trap Under wasn't exactly open to the public, and there weren't any city streets, but the service tunnels and access corridors and passageways linked up to form a web under the entire Trap, and most of it wasn't guarded or patrolled. Getting around wasn't a problem as long as you stayed clear of the high-security areas. Oh, there were cameras everywhere, but nobody ever bothered to check out most of what they picked up; they were for backtracking after an incident, not keeping an eye on everyone who took a shortcut through the tunnels.

I didn't expect any trouble getting to an entrance to Seventh Heaven's tank farm, and I didn't have any—a few minutes' walk, a ride down an open freight elevator, then another short walk, and there I was, standing in a black plastic corridor at a yellow door that had "Seventh Heaven Service Access T5" stenciled on it. No one bothered much with any sort of variable imaging on the basic labels down here; it was just paint, and didn't change at my approach.

The door didn't open, either.

I stood there for a moment, looking impatient, but if the door was watching me it didn't care; it didn't say anything. "Got a delivery," I said.

The door still didn't answer.

I frowned, and took another look—maybe it wasn't that smart a door. I didn't see any lenses or speakers, but that didn't mean anything. There was a big steel handle; I leaned on that, but it didn't budge.

There was also a red panel with white lettering that said "Emergency access—alarm will sound."

I considered that for a moment, and then decided I didn't care about setting off any alarms. It would mean I wouldn't have much time to explore before trouble showed up, and I might need to go ahead and get Dad out now instead of waiting, maybe make a run for it, but I was here, and I wanted to know if he was really in there. I slid the panel up, and found a single big red button behind it. I pressed it, hard, with my thumb.

Sure enough, an alarm sounded—a sort of hooting. I ignored it, and watched as the door shook slightly; then the latch released and the door slid open.

It had opened less than halfway when I slipped sideways past it into the tank farm.

The alarms were hooting in here, too, and red lights were flashing, though the regular lights were on, too.

"Please identify yourself," something said.

"Hu Xiao," I said. "Officer of the court, on city business." I was in a corridor, with rows of black panels set with video displays on either side—dreamtanks, I assumed. I had never seen one up close before.

The hooting stopped, but the red flashes didn't. "Please state the nature of your business."

"I'm investigating a reported kidnapping," I lied, trotting down the corridor.

At the first intersection I stopped and looked around for some indication of where I should go, and saw that the passage I was in was labeled T5, while the corridor crossing it was R1. I headed straight on.

At the next intersection Corridor T5 crossed Corridor R2. I smiled; that seemed straightforward enough, and picked up the pace.

"Please explain the nature of your investigation," the voice said, startling me. It had been quiet for so long I thought it had given up.

"Classified," I told it.

R3, R4...

"Human personnel have been contacted, and are on their way to discuss the situation," it said. "Please have your city ID ready."

"Of course," I said, and I drew the HG-2.

"Officer Hu, your appearance and voice do not match the information on file."

"Rejuve surgery," I said as I got to the corner of R6 and hesitated. "I need to update that." I picked a direction at random and turned right.

Bad choice. The intersections were much farther apart in this direction, so by the time I spotted the red T6 on the wall above the corner tank I could hear footsteps in the distance.

"Hello?" someone called. It sounded like a man, not a machine, but you can't always tell. "Officer Hu?"

"Over here," I called. "Row Five." I turned and hurried back down Row Six, hoping we wouldn't cross the Tier 5 corridor at the same time.

We didn't; a moment later the voice was behind me, calling, "Officer Hu?"

I was in Row 6, between the T4 and T5 corridors—did that put me in Tier 4? And which tank was Station 31? I didn't see any numbers.

"Officer Hu, if you don't show yourself I'll have to call Security."

"I'm over here," I said, while I wondered who I was talking to. Wasn't he Security? Did he mean he'd have to call for reinforcements? I stopped midway down the row and studied the nearest dreamtank's display panel. It was blank. I tapped it with a fingernail.

The word STANDBY appeared on the panel.

"Status report," I said.

"Officer Hu?"

"Right here," I called, as the screen lit up.

The red flashing lights were distracting, but I could read the screen. TIER 4, ROW 6, STATION 18, it said at the top. OHTA, AZRAEL—I took that to be the occupant's name. A screenful of data appeared below that—medical data, a list of recently-played dreams, and more. Azrael Ohta's blood glucose was 72 and his BP was 91 over 63, which both seemed a little low, but otherwise he appeared to be in good health, and he was eighty-three minutes into something called "Desert Encounter 306," with thirty-one minutes to go.

But he wasn't my father. I turned around and looked at the opposite side of the corridor. A tap on that panel got me the STANDBY message.

And then a paunchy guy in a purple turban and blue worksuit appeared at the corner of T5 and R6, looking at me.

"You're not Hu Xiao," he said

"Neither are you," I said, hoping to confuse him.

"I saw a picture," he said. "You aren't Officer Hu. Who are you? What are you doing here?"

I sighed, pressed the power button, and raised the HG-2. "I'm threatening you with a heavy-gravity handgun loaded with homing incendiaries," I said. "That's what I'm doing here. Now, are you going to cooperate, or is this going to get nasty?"

Chapter Twelve

H e raised his hands slowly and stared at me. "Who are you?" he asked.

"I'm the person with the gun," I told him, as I stepped away from the dreamtank and trained the HG-2 on his generously-sized belly. "That's all you need to know right now."

"You're trespassing."

"Oh, there's a shock," I said. "Did you think I hadn't noticed?"

"What do you want here? There's nothing worth stealing."

"Is that why you aren't armed?"

"Why would I be armed? I'm just maintenance."

"Not security?"

"No. Why would we have a human guard here? There's nothing worth stealing!"

"Security has been summoned," the room said.

"Tell them to stay back—there's a hostage situation," I said, keeping the gun pointed at the maintenance worker.

"They won't be here for twenty minutes anyway," my hostage said. "Our security is the casino cops from the Ginza, and they'll want to clear it with management before they come down here."

I considered that, then asked, "Why are you telling me?"

"Hey, you're pointing a gun at me. I don't want you getting nervous because things aren't going the way you expect them to."

That made sense. "Which of these is Station 31?" I asked, nodding toward the dreamtanks on my right. "Give me a hand, and I can be out of here before the casino cops ever show up. No danger of getting caught in the crossfire."

"Thirty-one?" He blinked, then pointed, keeping his hand high as he did. "Over there somewhere." The hands drooped a little. "Is that what you're after? One of these lose... I mean, one of our clients?"

"That's right. Can you get him out for me?"

"You gonna kill him?"

I grimaced. "No," I said. Then a memory of what it had felt like when the three of us got the news that our parents were dumping us stirred in the back of my head somewhere, and I added, "Though he maybe deserves it."

"He owes you money?" He shook his head. "He can't pay it. That's part of the deal. The company takes control of all assets and all debts when the babies go in the bottle. They give up control of their own affairs. If he has any money left, he can't touch it."

"I know that!" I snapped. "I'm not here to...never mind. Just open Station 31, will you? It's none of your business what I want with him."

He shrugged. "Sure. No juice out of *my* system." He lowered his hands and headed toward one of the tanks. He tapped the display and said, "Maintenance."

The screen lit up. He glanced at it and said, "Oops." He moved two panels over and repeated his performance, except this time instead of "oops," he said, "Got it."

I moved cautiously closer, keeping the gun ready and staying a couple of meters out of reach.

TIER 4, ROW 6, STATION 31, the top line of the display read, and the second line said HSING, GUOHAN.

That was him.

"Huh," the maintenance worker said. "Is that spelled right?"

"Yes," I said. "Get him out."

"I mean, it's usually Singh, S I N G H. That's how I spell it. Maybe the H is in the wrong place."

I put that together with the guy's turban. "He's not a Sikh," I said. "The name's Chinese, with an archaic spelling. Now, get him out of there."

"I don't know if that's a good idea," the turbaned man—presumably Mis' Singh—said.

"Security is on its way," the room reminded us. "Please do not take any hasty actions."

"Get him out," I repeated.

"He's been in there a long time," the maintenance worker warned me. "If I get him out he's going to be pretty disoriented, and there's probably been some muscle atrophy."

I hadn't really thought that through. I knew he might not be feeling very cooperative after being snatched out of his mechanical womb, away from his pretty fantasies, but that was one reason I'd brought the gun. That he might not be able to walk could complicate matters.

I couldn't take the whole tank; it was too big, and built into the floor. It wasn't designed to move. I had to get my father out, and if he couldn't walk, that was a problem.

Fortunately, I had a solution standing right there.

"You may need to carry him for me, then," I said. "Don't worry, he's not a big man."

"After all those years in there, I'll bet he's not." He glanced around. "Carry him *where*?"

"Anywhere I can get a cab."

He looked baffled. "You're taking him away with you? Why? He's a dreamer, nobody's going to ransom him or anything."

"I know that."

"Does he know something you want? Are you planning to question him? Because there might be some memory loss..."

"You ask a lot of questions for someone being held at gunpoint," I said. "Just get him out." I pressed a button on the HG-

2, and it made a threatening whine, as if the targeting mechanism were adjusting.

The real targeting mechanism was completely silent, of course; the button was just sound effects.

The sound effects worked, though; Mis' Singh, if that was his name, stopped asking questions and got busy with the panel on T4 R6 S31. A moment later there was a hiss, then a whir, and then Station 31 opened and a bed slid out.

And there was my father, lying naked in the bed—not on it, but sunk down into it, surrounded by worn brown plastic. He was curled into fetal position, lying on his left side, but going by the wear on the plastic, and the condition of his skin, he had been turned every so often. Tubes ran into both arms, his mouth, nose, anus, and urethra; a visor covered his eyes, and a heavy-duty cable was plugged into the back of his skull and secured with a clamp around his throat. He was shriveled and shrunken, his skin dry and flaking, his hair long and ragged; the only part of him that still looked healthy and normal was the wire job on his neck and one side of his head.

I hadn't seen him in years, and when I did he hadn't looked like this, he'd been healthy and alert, but all the same, I recognized him immediately. This was Guohan Hsing, all right. This was my father, genetically if not legally.

"Get him out of there," I said again. The maintenance guy tapped the control panel; the throat clamp released with a sharp click, and tubes started withdrawing. I decided I didn't need to watch that, and focused my attention on the paunchy man's face, but I could *hear* the tubes sliding from their places, which was almost as bad.

"Do you want him awake?" Singh asked.

"Waking Mis' Hsing is a violation of his contract," the room said. "Please wait for Security before taking further action."

"I just want him alive," I said. "Awake or asleep doesn't really matter right now."

"Waking Mis' Hsing is a violation of his contract," the voice repeated.

"Can you shut that thing off?" I asked Singh. I gestured with the gun. "It's annoying me."

"Not from here," the maintenance worker said.

"It's not very bright."

"It doesn't have to be, to watch over a bunch of dreamers."

The hiss and gurgle of retracting tubes stopped, and I heard the rasping as my father began breathing unassisted for the first time in years. I hesitated before looking at him, though; I wasn't sure I really wanted to see him.

"They didn't give it much authority, did they?" I said, putting off the inevitable. "You didn't need to do anything to override it."

"You just said it's not very bright, Mis'. Would you trust it with anyone's life?"

Then Dad coughed, a harsh, choking cough, and I turned to help.

So did the maintenance guy. Between us we got my father into a sitting position as he choked and gasped, his lungs struggling to work unaided. He coughed uncontrollably for what seemed like half an hour, but which my symbiote told me was only about twenty seconds, and when he was finally able to stop he was wide awake, sitting in his plastic bed. He raised one trembling hand and lifted off the visor, then looked up at us.

He tried to talk, but all that came out was a wheeze, and that started him coughing again. I decided not to wait. "Pick him up," I told Singh. I had lowered the gun while we moved my father; now I pointed it again.

He hesitated, glancing at Dad. "What are you going to do with him?" he asked.

"I'm going to get him off Epimetheus before sunrise," I said. "Pick him up!"

"Security will arrive in approximately eighty-five seconds," the room said. "Please stand by."

"Off-planet? How?" Singh asked.

"I have a ship," I said. "It's waiting at the port. Unless you want to get caught in the crossfire, I suggest you pick him up and get him out of here before those fifteen seconds are up."

Singh took maybe half a second to think it over, then nodded. He bent down, tugged the loose clamp out of the way, unplugged the cable from the back of Dad's neck, then slid his arms under shoulders and knees and picked my father up. Either the maintenance guy was stronger than he looked, or Dad weighed about as much as a cup of tea. He put up about as much resistance as a tea cup, too.

"Which way?" Singh asked.

"Out," I said. "Wherever Security isn't. You show me."

He nodded and began walking, and said, "What kind of ship?"

"A yacht," I said, following him. I had to trot to keep up. "Not mine."

"Room for another passenger?"

I should have expected that. "If it won't get me arrested, there might be."

"Hey, getting me out isn't anywhere *near* as illegal as kidnapping this poor guy I'm carrying."

"Stop right there!" a new voice called.

I turned, the HG-2 in my hand, but before I could say anything Singh called, "It's okay, guys!"

I didn't point the gun at anyone after all; instead I just looked at the two cops who were coming down the aisle toward us. They had guns, too—nothing quite as big as the HG-2, but probably more than enough to kill me several times over. A floater was hanging just above and behind them, scanning the scene.

"What's wrong?" I said, trying to sound confused.

"The surveillance system here reported a hostage situation," the lead cop said, keeping his gun trained on me. The second cop, I noticed, was pointing *his* gun at Singh.

Singh had been telling the truth about Seventh Heaven's security; these two were in charcoal-gray suits with the Ginza logo on the breast and security badges on their sleeves. Casino cops—that was both good and bad. Good, because they didn't really care about the law, only about what was good for business, and shooting potential customers was pretty much never good for business. Bad, because they not only didn't care whether *I* was breaking the law, they didn't care whether *they* were, either—they could play rough.

"The surveillance system is an idiot," Singh said. "There's a maintenance problem, that's all—I had to get this poor loser out before his tank poisoned him."

"Who are you?"

Singh sighed. "I'm Minish Singh, second-shift maintenance."

"Who's she?"

"Hu Xiao. She wanted me to check on this guy—he's a potential witness. Good thing she did; he'd have been dead in an hour."

I thought that was pretty good improvisation; I wondered whether they'd buy it. I didn't think *I* would have, but I'm not a casino cop. Casino cops don't like trouble.

"Surveillance, can you confirm?"

"Minish Singh, confirmed. However, this person does not match city records of Hu Xiao."

"I told you, rejuve," I said. "My files need updating."

"She's Officer Hu," Singh said.

"She threatened Mis' Singh with what she called a heavy-gravity handgun loaded with homing incendiaries," the room said. I thought it sounded...miffed, maybe. Or pettish. One of those strange old words that shouldn't apply to a half-witted piece of software.

"Fine, my weapon isn't standard issue," I said. "Is that any of your concern?"

"You threatened him?" the lead cop asked.

"What?" I tried to look innocent. "No, I didn't *threaten* him, I just told him to hurry."

The second cop spoke for the first time. "Who's the corpse?" he asked.

"I'm not..." Dad said. Then his voice gave out, and he coughed instead of finishing the sentence.

"Guohan Hsing," Singh said.

"He's a potential witness in a kidnap," I said, trying to reconcile the story I'd given the room with the story Singh had made up.

"I'm not dead," Dad said. This time he got the whole thing out, but so quietly I'm not sure the cops heard him.

They didn't care, in any case. To them he was a body Seventh Heaven had been storing, and whether he was alive or dead was a technical detail that didn't interest them.

"His tank glitched," Singh said.

"Or was hacked," I said.

"Surveillance, who's the hostage here?" the less-talkative cop asked.

"The intruder calling herself Hu Xiao was holding Mis' Singh at gunpoint."

"Oh, come on," I said. "I was just trying to hurry him a little. Who wrote this piece of gritware, anyway? I'm sorry to drag you two down here, guys—I guess this surveillance system's a little buggy."

"Mis' Singh, was this woman threatening you?" the lead cop asked.

"No," my father and Singh said in unison.

The second cop smiled at that, and lowered his gun a little.

"May we please get this man out of here to someplace he can get medical attention?" Singh demanded. "This is all a misunderstanding, but that tank *did* almost kill him."

"I did not detect any malfunction," the room said, and I had to agree it wasn't a very good piece of software—it made this statement in a flat tone, neither sulky nor defensive. That trace of emotion I thought I'd detected before was gone.

"Well, I have eyes, not just a datafeed," Singh said. "Something glitched his tank. We need to get him out of here."

"And after that Mis' Vo wants to question him," I said. I thought whoever was listening to the bugs in my gun, assuming someone was, might be amused by that.

The lead cop glanced over his shoulder at the floater. "Any advice? Orders?"

"Neither account is entirely consistent or believable," the floater said in a pleasant alto

"So *everyone's* lying?"

"Or mistaken."

"You think it's all a misunderstanding?"

"We have insufficient evidence to conclude otherwise."

"I don't want to get mixed up in a kidnapping," the second cop said.

"Look, I'm the ranking representative of Seventh Heaven here," Singh said. "I'm telling you there's no problem. Go on back to the Ginza and forget about it."

"What the hell," the lead cop said, holstering his pistol. "That runs smooth enough for me."

"Want us to file a bug report?" the second asked Singh.

"I'll take care of it," he replied.

A second floater had arrived, I noticed. I didn't say anything, and tried not to let anyone see I had noticed it; it was stealthed, hiding itself in a holo that blended with the ceiling.

Except it had set the holo up as a compromise, angled as best it could to fool all three of us—Singh, Dad, and me. And I was shorter and closer than they were, so my angle was different, and the image wasn't aligned perfectly for me.

"Good enough," the cop said. He holstered his weapon, as well, and the two of them turned away. The big floater, the visible one, kept a lens trained on us to make sure we didn't try anything, and followed the two humans as they headed back the way they had come.

For a second or two Singh and I watched them go; then Singh said, "Come on," and started walking again. He shifted my father around into a more comfortable position; it really looked as if my old man didn't weigh more than a dozen kilos.

"Just a moment," I said. "Let me check the safety." I looked down at the HG-2, and at the image of the ceiling reflected on the inert diagnostics screen.

The stealthed floater was still there. I activated the gun's targeting system, hoping it could find the floater and lock onto it. Then I hurried after the maintenance worker.

I had to be careful what I said, since I knew we were being watched. I couldn't even safely *tell* Singh we were being watched, not with both the stealthed floater and the bugged gun listening in.

"Thanks," I said.

"Hey, if you can really..."

I interrupted him. "You aren't happy here?" I said.

He glanced back at me, puzzled. Then he looked thoughtfully along Row 6.

He might not see the floater, but he knew we could be heard. The surveillance system might be stupid, but it was probably bright enough to record everything, and sooner or later it would send those recordings to someone or something that *wasn't* stupid.

It probably had enough recorded already to get us both sent for reconstruction if anyone decided to push. There was no point in pretending we were complete innocents.

But we didn't want to say anything that would get us moved to the top of the priority list, either.

"No, I'm not happy," he said. He waved at the dreamtanks around us. "Look around. You know what people call us, all of us who work here?"

I knew. "Corpsefuckers," I said.

"That's right," he said angrily. "You look at this son of a bitch I'm carrying. Never mind that he's not dead, you think anyone would want to screw that?"

I didn't want to look at him. I wanted to remember my father as a human being, not a dessicated ruin. "I don't think anyone means it literally," I said. "It's just... it seems creepy, working with all these comatose dreamers."

"It *is* creepy," Singh agreed. "Not to mention boring—no one's buying dreams anymore, not when the city's about to fry, and I'm nothing but a back-up system, watching the machines tend a bunch of losers nobody cares about. You know something, Mis' One-With-the-Gun? I've had enough of it. If you can get me somewhere I can find a better job, I'll do whatever you want with this Guohan Hsing. Do you know where you're taking him?"

"I'm headed for American City on Prometheus," I said. "Or maybe Alderstadt."

"Either one sounds good to me."

"What..." The voice was a dry whisper, but we both heard it. "Who are you people?" my father asked.

"My name's Minish Singh," the paunchy guy said, without stopping. I hoped he knew where he was going. "Until maybe five minutes ago I was the second shift maintenance crew for Seventh Heaven Neurosurgery."

"What are you doing with me? This is *real*, isn't it?"

"As real as it gets," Singh replied.

"Why? I paid for a lifetime contract!"

"Ask her," Singh said, nodding over his shoulder toward me.

Dad struggled to turn his head to look at me, but the neck muscles weren't strong enough. Singh shifted his hold to help, and my father stared at me.

"You look familiar," he said at last.

"Good to know," I answered.

"You look...how long has it been?"

"Long enough," I said.

"You're Carlie, aren't you? Or... Ali? Or a granddaughter?"

"Right the first time," I told him.

"Carlie?" There was a sort of wonder in his voice—and apprehension. "Are you going to kill me?"

"Why the hell would I do that?" I snapped. "Seems to me you already did it for me!"

"You...you might want revenge for dumping you," he said. "I thought... I've..." He began coughing again, and Singh thumped him on the back as if he was burping a baby.

Then we were at a door, and Singh pressed his thumb on the screen and the door slid open, and we were in a service corridor, black plastic all around. I glanced up where I thought the stealthed floater probably was, but I couldn't spot it.

I'd want to do something about that.

I tapped my wrist to call for a cab, then told Dad, "If I wanted you dead, you'd be dead. If I wanted you to suffer, you'd be suffering. You think no one can tamper with the software here? *Anything* can be hacked, you know that."

"We need to find street access," Singh said. "The cabs can't get in here."

"Scroll us out," I told him.

"Where are you taking me?" my father asked, as Singh turned left and trotted down the corridor. Dad's voice was still weak, every word coming with an effort.

"Prometheus," I said, hurrying to keep up. "Where you can go right back into a dreamtank. Don't worry, I'm not trying to get you to take your life back; I just don't trust Seventh Heaven to keep things running after the city's fried."

"Is your mother there? On Prometheus?"

"What? Of course not. She's been out-system for years."

"Then why?"

I wasn't any too sure of that myself. "Because someone offered to get you off-planet, and it seemed like a good play at the time," I said.

"But we *dumped* you."

"I know that, you bastard," I said. I could feel my eyes welling up. "God damn it, I know that. But you never asked whether *we* intended to dump *you*."

Chapter Thirteen

We came out in a maintenance shaft—it wasn't street level, but it was open to the sky and a cab could get in. I beeped for one. Then I looked at the HG-2 and checked the read-outs to see if it had a fix on the invisible floater.

It did. I lifted the gun, pointed it in the right general direction, and fired.

The recoil knocked me back against the shaft wall, so I didn't get a good view of the explosion, but what I saw was pretty damned satisfying. Scraps of hot metal and melted plastic rattled off the walls and floor, and sparking bits of electronics spattered in all directions.

"What the *hell*...?" Singh said, turning around fast. He dropped my father on the way.

"Spy-eye," I said. "The Ginza cops set it on us."

"And you *killed* it?"

"Yes," I said. I didn't say anything more than that aloud, but I was thinking that I really hoped it hadn't been sentient. I had quite enough to explain to my ancestors when the time came without adding another murder.

"That blast is going to get the *city* cops after us!"

"*Pfui*," I said. "When was the last time you saw city cops do anything down here?"

"You've sure as hell pissed off the Ginza!"

I shrugged. "I've been on their gritlist for years."

A weird hissing noise interrupted us, and we both turned to see where it was coming from.

My father was lying sprawled on the floor of the shaft, laughing at us.

"My Carlie," he said. "Look at you!"

"I look a hell of a lot better than you do," I retorted.

"You...you're living like one of my dreams," he said. "How did *that* happen?"

"My parents did the dump on me when I was fifteen," I said, and I knew I sounded bitter and sarcastic, and I didn't care. "I learned to do whatever I had to do to survive."

"You're...what, an assassin?"

"A private detective," I said.

"And you're taking me to Prometheus?"

"Shut up," I replied; something was moving overhead, and I wanted to be sure it was our cab, and not a Ginza enforcer.

Then it was sinking down the shaft with the headlights blazing, a cloud of stardust forming the Midnight Cab & Limo logo on its taxi-yellow belly. "Our ride's here," I said.

"So are those," Singh said, pointing.

I looked where his finger indicated, and spotted two glossy black floaters—not stealthed, but not lit, either. They were big ones, probably weighed more inert than I did, and were heading directly toward us. I didn't see a logo—not the Ginza's, not the city cops' insignia, nothing but gleaming black. They didn't look like newsies; there were no visible lenses or antennas.

I looked at my gun and thought about it, but there were two of them, and they might be armed. I could maybe take out one before they could react, but there was no way I could get them both, and I didn't know what the survivor would be capable of.

They weren't shooting at us, and they weren't shouting, so I decided we could ignore them for the moment.

Well, partially ignore them, anyway. They did force me to change my plans. I had originally hoped to call 'Chan, get him to the casino door, then grab him, maybe drug him, and haul him along to the ship. That would have gotten everyone together, one happy family, and we could have just taken off for American City before the cops could stop us.

With those floaters there watching us, that probably wasn't going to work.

"Someone called for a cab?" the Midnight cab called, its door sliding open as it hung a few centimeters off the deck.

"Get him in," I told Singh, pointing at my father. While he loaded Dad into the cab I watched the black floaters, but they had slowed to a stop. They were hovering silently at the top of the shaft, noses toward us.

"You coming?" Singh called. He and Dad were sitting in the cab, the door open.

I holstered the HG-2 and climbed in after them. The door was closing behind me when a Ginza floater, exactly like the one that had accompanied the cops—in fact, it probably *was* the one that had accompanied the cops—came dropping down toward us.

"Transparency," I told the cab. "I want to see this."

The roof seemed to vanish, and there was the Ginza floater, swooping down toward us—and then the black floaters were moving again, as well.

But they weren't moving toward the cab; they were diving in to cut off the Ginza's floater.

"Get us out of here," I said.

"I don't want any trouble with the casino," the cab protested.

"Neither do we," I said, "but it looks as if someone else does." The black floaters had blocked the cop's approach.

I couldn't see the Ginza floater anymore, since the black floaters were easily twice its size and there were two of them between us, but the cab had its external audio on, so I could hear it.

"Hu Xiao!" the Ginza floater called. "You are charged with the destruction of casino property!"

"I don't want any trouble with the casino," the cab repeated.

"And I told you, we don't either," I said. "None of us is this Hu Xiao person. See for yourself." I slid my card in the slot.

"Thank you, Mis' Hsing," it said. "And these others?"

Singh threw me a glance, then fished out his own card and tabbed it in.

"Thank you. And the last of you?"

"That's my father, Guohan Hsing," I said. "He doesn't have his card with him, but if you're set up for a DNA check you can verify it."

"I'm Guohan Hsing," Dad agreed. "You can check my voiceprint if you can't do a genetic scan."

I wasn't any too sure his scratchy whisper would match any old voiceprints the cab might have access to, but apparently the cab was convinced somehow; it began rising.

"I notice the elder Mis' Hsing is naked and does not appear entirely well," it said, as it cleared the lip of the shaft. "Is medical attention desired?"

I was watching the floaters and almost didn't hear it; the Ginza floater was still trying to get at us, and the black floaters were blocking it, forcing it back. "Who *are* those things?" I asked.

Then the cab's question registered, and I quickly added, "Thank you, but no medical attention is needed. Just get us to the port asap."

"The blue floater is a security unit owned by the Ginza Casino Hotel," the cab said, answering my question. "The other two are refusing all requests for identification, but the specifications match descriptions of high-level units owned by the New York Townhouse Hotel and Gambling Hall."

"Carlisle Hsing!" the Ginza floater called. "You are charged with destruction of casino property and giving a false name to security personnel!"

They'd ID'ed me. I was a bit surprised it had taken that long, but I wasn't really thinking about that. I was thinking about the black floaters. They belonged to the New York?

That meant they belonged to the Nakadas. Had Grandfather Nakada sent them to protect me? It didn't seem likely; it didn't seem like his style, and besides, everyone on Epimetheus thought he was dead. He couldn't just give orders and expect them to be carried out without any explanation of his reported demise.

But who else could have sent them? Obviously, someone who'd been listening in—maybe through my gun, maybe through datafeed from Seventh Heaven or the casino cops—but who would have cared enough to send this pair?

I didn't understand what was happening, and I didn't like that. I wasn't going to take any more big risks until I had a better idea what was running.

"The port," I told the cab. "Hurry!"

"But the Ginza..."

"We aren't in their jurisdiction," I said. "Go!"

"I'm going."

It was; we soared up out of the shaft, and up Sixth Street, then diagonally over the rooftops toward the port.

"Oh, gods!" my father said.

I turned, thinking something was wrong, thinking maybe his heart was giving out without the steady stream of meds and fluids he'd had in the tank, but no, if anything he was looking better than ever. He was sitting up and staring out at the city.

Specifically, he was staring at the western wall of the crater, where the morning sun was gradually creeping downward from the rim, and at the higher towers, where sunlight was gleaming from their top few floors..

"It's the dawn," he said. "It is, isn't it?"

"Not yet," Singh told him.

"Soon, though," I said. "That's why I'm getting you out. I expect Seventh Heaven to declare bankruptcy the minute that light hits the streets of Trap Over. Maybe they won't just leave all the dreamers to rot in their tanks, but I didn't want to take the risk."

"How long was I in there?" Dad asked.

I glared at him. "I was sixteen, almost seventeen, when you went in," I said. "Look at me now."

"It's *horrible*," he said. "So bright!"

I almost laughed. I'd spent a year on Prometheus. I'd even been stranded on the Epimethean dayside once. To me, Nightside City was still an island of comforting darkness, even if the sky was no longer black. "What, none of your dreams were out in the sun?" I asked.

"Some of them were, yes, but those weren't *real*. I always knew that. And they weren't in Nightside City, in my *home*."

"Your home is about to get hit with hard ultraviolet," I said. "The temperature's already climbed at least ten degrees, and it hasn't rained since you bought your dream. You knew that was coming."

"I...I knew it, but I didn't *believe* it."

I snorted. "So you ran and hid in a dreamworld where you wouldn't have to see it," I said. "You know, when I pulled you out, I wasn't sure whether you would wake up or not, but I'm glad you did, so you could see this."

"I don't like it," he said. "I want to go back."

"Too late for that," Singh muttered.

"No, it isn't," I said. "I could drop the two of you, you could tell the authorities I had you at gunpoint the whole time and you never wanted to cooperate, and you could take Mis' Hsing here back to his happy fantasy life in the tank."

Singh looked at me. "And what do *you* do?"

"I get back to the port and head for Prometheus, and hope my rich friends there can buy my way out of this mess."

"And what about those?" He pointed.

I followed his finger to where the two big black floaters were following us at a frighteningly small distance, maybe ten meters behind our cab. "Oh," I said.

I didn't know who sent those two, which meant I didn't know what they would or wouldn't interfere with. They might not let me dump anyone, or flee anywhere.

There was no sign of the Ginza cop floater, though. That was something. I wondered whether the black ones had disabled it somehow, or whether it had realized it was outmatched and backed down, or whether it had been called back by the casino management.

Any of those was possible.

Who *had* sent the black floaters? Were they helping me, or just keeping me for themselves?

I didn't think Yoshio had sent them. If he had, wouldn't they have told me? But if he hadn't, who had? Was someone from the New York tracking me? If so, was it at Vo's direction, or without his knowledge?

Or was someone keeping an eye on the Seventh Heaven dreamtanks?

Nakada floaters, according to the cab. And it was presumably a Nakada who had used the back door into Seventh Heaven's data. If someone *was* keeping an eye on them, it was a Nakada, or at any rate someone with access to the clan's inner workings.

And someone with access to the clan's inner workings had tried to kill Grandfather Nakada. Someone had made copies of the old man's ITEOD files, including back-ups of a dozen high-ranking Nakadas.

I didn't think Vo had anything to do with it.

It might all be coincidence. It might be unrelated intrigues or corporate espionage. I didn't think that was the way to bet it. It looked to me as if it was all part of the same conspiracy, and the only coincidence—if it *was* a coincidence, and not somehow connected—was that the dream company involved happened to be the same one that had my father tucked away in their tanks.

Dreams—someone was monitoring the top dream company on Epimetheus, and someone had tried to kill Yoshio Nakada by tampering with his dream enhancer. Another link.

But it wasn't about me or my father at all, then, and I could still try to grab my brother.

"Wait a minute," I told the cab. "Can you get back to the Ginza without attracting any unwanted attention?"

"What?" Singh said. "I thought we were heading for this ship of yours, to get the hell off Epimetheus!"

"There's another passenger," I said. "Someone else I want to bring."

"Where are you planning to *put* her?" Singh demanded. "This thing's full!"

It didn't look that full to me; yes, there were three of us on the main seat, but there was a luggage compartment in the rear, and I suspected a second seat could be folded up. "Cab, how many passengers are you licensed for?"

"Six, mis'."

"Then can you get back to the Ginza?"

"I don't know, mis'," it said. "Those two floaters are following me, and I'm on the navigation grid; if anyone wants to find us, they can."

"I thought you were in a hurry!" Singh protested.

"My brother's in the Ginza," I said.

"Sebastian?" Dad croaked. He was slumped against the side of the passenger compartment, staring out through the transparent bubble at the glittering ads that filled the streets of Trap Over.

"Yes, Sebastian," I told him. "He's a croupier."

Dad lifted his head from the plastic. "I'd like to see him," he said.

Just then Singh's com buzzed. He tapped it for speaker.

"Minish Singh," he said.

"Singh," it replied, in a woman's voice, "what the hell is going on?"

"Damned if I know," Singh said.

"That woman you're with has been identified as a private investigator named Carlisle Hsing, except Hsing is supposed to be off-planet, on Prometheus. Do you have any idea who she really is?"

"She gave her name as Hu Xiao," Singh said, throwing me a questioning look.

"She's not Hu Xiao—at least, not the court officer Hu Xiao."

"Then I don't know any more than you do."

"She's listening to this, isn't she?"

"Yes, mis'."

For a moment no one spoke; then the cab asked, "Am I supposed to be going to the port or the Ginza?"

"The Ginza," I told it. Then I told Singh's com, "I'm Carlisle Hsing. My brother Sebastian can identify me. He's a croupier at the Ginza."

"I'm assistant director of security for the Ginza, Mis'. I know Sebastian Hsing."

"Then you can arrange for him to talk to me."

"I could, yes, but why should I?"

"Because I asked nicely?"

She sighed. "Mis' Hsing, what do you think you're doing? According to the records you've occasionally cut a few corners, but you've basically stayed clean. Now you've shot a floater and kidnapped an attendant and someone from a dreamtank, not to mention trespassing, avoiding arrest, impersonating an officer—what is this?"

"It's a misunderstanding."

"It's one hell of a misunderstanding."

"Let me talk to my brother, face to face, and I'll explain. We're on our way back to straighten this out."

She didn't answer right away. Then she said, "I'll need to check with the floor manager."

"You do that," I said. "Oh, but one question first."

"What?"

"That floater I shot, the stealthed one—what kind was it?"

"What do you mean, what kind?"

"Was it sentient?"

"Not really. Semi-autonomous."

"Thank you." I leaned back on the seat, and only when I did that did I realize I'd been hunched forward. Now I could relax a little. "You go ask whoever you need to ask."

I had assumed it was just a dumb tracker when I first shot it, but then I'd had second thoughts. It was good to know I had been right the first time. Legally it probably didn't make any difference, but it mattered to *me* whether I'd killed something self-aware.

For the most part I was making this up as I went, as I usually did, but I decided it was time to do a little advance planning, for once. I ran my fingers over my wrist and sent a little message to the *Ukiba*—four words, "add a hot lunch." I was fairly certain Yoshio-*kun* would punctuate that properly, even if Perkins didn't—add "a" to "hot lunch," and have a hot launch ready to go when we got back to the ship.

"Privacy," I told the cab, once the message showed as sent and received.

The view of the surrounding city vanished instantly as the cab went opaque, and my symbiote flashed an alarm that all external input and net access had been cut off.

"Thanks," I said. "Tab yourself a fat tip for this—double the fare, if you want." I might as well enjoy my expense account while I could.

"Thank you, mis'," it replied. "It's very exciting!"

"I thought you didn't want any trouble," I said, amused.

"It seems as if I have it whether I want it or not, so I might as well enjoy it."

I grimaced. I wished that attitude was more common.

Then I turned my attention to Singh and my father. "Listen," I said, "they think I kidnapped you two, but I really *am* going to kidnap my brother 'Chan. He's got an implant that'll shut down his legs if he leaves the Ginza, so we'll need to carry him. Once he's off-planet we can get the implant out, but first we need to get him onto the ship. Dad, I know you're in no shape to do anything, but Singh, can you help me with this?"

Singh cocked his head. "How big is your brother?" he asked.

"Bigger then me," I said. "Bigger than my father. But not really big."

"What's in it for me?"

"Besides a ride to Prometheus?"

"Yes, besides that."

I glared at him, then shrugged. "A kilocredit."

"Five."

"Two-five."

"Three."

"Done."

We shook hands, and then loaded my father into the luggage compartment, where he would be safely out of the way.

"Everything hurts," he complained. "I feel every little bump, and my legs and hands are all stiff."

"That's how you know you're alive," I said.

"They didn't hurt in the dream."

"It wouldn't be much of a dream if they did," Singh said, as he straightened Dad's limbs to make him more comfortable.

"We're approaching the Ginza," the cab said.

"Let me see," I said, and as the bubble turned transparent and the city reappeared around us, I pulled my gun from its holster and tapped the power switch to on.

Chapter Fourteen

I hadn't specified which entrance to use, so the cab had brought us down at the big front door on Cassiopeia Avenue, and our arrival was the central act of a circus.

Ginza cops were everywhere, three or four different varieties of them, and a few characters who had the look of cops but who I didn't think were from the Ginza. People in fancy suits were there, as well, and I don't think they were all on the same side. Dozens of floaters were swooping around, or hovering—newsies and security and spy-eyes, and advertisers that saw a crowd forming and didn't care why. Tourists were watching; they probably had no idea what was going on, but thought it looked exciting.

Add that to the usual glittering chaos of a casino's entrance, the stardust and holos and lightscapes.

But I didn't see 'Chan.

"Hey," I said into Singh's com. "Where's my brother?"

"On his way."

"We'll wait."

The cab asked, "Will you be disembarking?"

"We're staying right where we are," I told it. "Go ahead and charge waiting rates if you want."

"Thank you, Mis'."

"You're either crazy, desperate, rich, or on an expense account," Singh remarked. "I'm guessing it's an expense account. You're working for someone."

"Could be more than one of those," I said.

"It could. You said something about rich friends; I'm betting it's more like a rich client."

I glanced at him. "You know, you should be careful about what you bet on. You might make someone angry."

"You must know you couldn't get out of this with your brain intact if you didn't have some pretty serious backing."

"So maybe I *want* to be reconstructed. Maybe it's my way of avoiding reality, since I can't afford to buy the dream the way my old man did."

Singh shook his head. "You aren't *that* crazy."

The cab was now completely surrounded by Ginza cops and security floaters. "Are you sure?" I asked.

He considered that for a moment, then said, "Yeah, I think I am."

"Good. Cab, privacy, please?"

"You do know that the city police can override my privacy field?"

"I didn't, but I'll risk it. Do it."

"Yes, mis'." The bubble went black, plunging us into gloom lit only by the cab's various internal displays.

I turned back to Singh. "Here's what I want you to do for your three kilocredits. I'm going to talk to my brother, and I'm going to tell him I have someone here in the cab he needs to see. He'll come over to look and he'll see our dad here—and when he does, you grab him and pull him into the cab."

"I can do that."

"And cabbie, the instant our new passenger is aboard, I want you to close up and head for the port as fast as you can. Don't wait for further instructions. Got it?"

"Yes, mis'."

"Good. Then drop the privacy."

"Yes, mis'." The bubble was transparent again, and I looked out at a dozen guns pointed at us—and at 'Chan, who was walking slowly across the entry plaza toward us. A woman in a navy blue suit was walking beside him and talking while read-outs flickered across her chest and sleeve. 'Chan was leaning toward her slightly, obviously listening to whatever she was saying.

"Open the door," I said.

The cab's door slid aside, and I perched myself in the opening with the HG-2 in my hand. "'Chan!" I called.

"Mis' Hsing," the woman beside him called. "Come out and talk."

"Talk first," I said. "Then maybe I'll come out." As I spoke I was trying to take in as much of my surroundings as possible, and in particular what sort of weaponry the casino cops were displaying. It looked like about half lethal, half merely incapacitating, which meant that they'd be willing to take me down at the first opportunity. Killing me would mean kiloscreens of reports and documentation and trouble with superiors who might want to know what the hell I'd thought I was doing, but tranking me, or otherwise shutting me down somehow, would be good for a few karma points, so long as I didn't manage to do any damage going down.

Which was why I had the gun turned on and ready. If they shot me I intended to get off a shot or two of my own before I went blank.

"Carlie, what the hell are you doing?" 'Chan asked. He sounded both concerned and annoyed.

"Did they tell you who I kidnapped?" I called.

'Chan glanced at his keeper—I wasn't sure if she was his boss as a security admin, or in a different chain of command, or what. "No," he called back.

"I think you should take a look."

The woman in blue whispered something to him; he threw her a startled glance.

"It may not be who they think it is," I said.

"Carlie, this is insane," he answered.

"Come take a look, and then tell me that."

That definitely had his interest; he came and looked. I leaned aside and pointed toward the luggage compartment.

"Is that Dad?" 'Chan asked, leaning in. "They said..."

And that was when Singh grabbed him by the front of his worksuit and heaved him over me into the cab.

"Go!" I shouted, but I didn't really need to; the cab was already moving.

The door closed on 'Chan's foot at first; we must have been forty meters up by the time the cab was able to get it free and Singh managed to pull 'Chan entirely in.

"I'm being ordered to land immediately," the cab told us.

"You tell 'em that if you land, I'll start shooting."

"They want to know whether I consider this a credible threat."

"I have an active gun here; what do *you* think?"

"I think I am not programmed for threat assessment. I am reporting this conclusion to the city police."

"It's *city* cops now?"

"Yes, mis'."

That was bad. I didn't want to mess with city cops. I glanced out through the bubble at the city zipping past. "Is this your maximum velocity?"

"I am exceeding the posted speed limits by the customary twenty-five percent."

"Go to emergency maximum, please."

"I am forbidden to do so without an order from authorized personnel."

"An active gun doesn't constitute authorization?"

"I regret to say it does not."

I looked out and saw no fewer than four cop cars following us —and those two black floaters. The cops seemed to be ignoring the floaters; I wasn't sure what to make of that.

Getting from the cab into the ship was going to be tricky.

"Privacy," I said.

"The city police have overridden my privacy systems."

Damn. "They're listening?"

"I would assume so."

I only had to think for a second. "Listen, cab," I said. "I like you, and I don't want you to get hurt. Put us down where I point, and as soon as we're out, get the hell out of there. You understand?"

"Yes, mis'."

"We're clear on the fare and tip?"

"I believe so, mis'."

I smiled. I did like this cab. "If you're coding for even more— well, how much can you take without getting called for an ethics violation?"

"You might be surprised, mis'."

I smiled wider. It even had something like a sense of humor— and maybe a sense of honor, too, giving me a graceful way to avoid wasting *too* much money. "I might, at that. Okay, not that much, but I'm feeling generous. You charge what seems fair."

"Thank you, mis'."

We were approaching the port by then. I tried to arrange myself so that my gestures wouldn't be visible to the cops behind us, but I knew the onboard security cams would be feeding to them, and they could calculate from those. "Put us down there," I said, pointing at the steps to *Ukiba*'s airlock.

"Yes, mis'."

"Carlie!" 'Chan said. "What the hell are you doing?"

I turned to look at him; he and Singh were thoroughly tangled on the seat beside me. Dad was leaning over the seat-back and grinning at them.

"Getting you out," I said. I would have said "off this planet" if the cops hadn't been listening. "Mis' Singh, can you manage both?"

Singh had straightened himself out. He looked at 'Chan and Dad, considering. He did not look happy.

"Never mind," I said. "Get him." I pointed at 'Chan. "I'll get the other."

"Carlie, you know the implant kicked in, and I'm paralyzed from the hips down, right?"

"I know," I said. "You just cooperate and no one gets hurt."

"Oh, come on, Carlie, I'm your brother! You aren't..." He stopped in mid-sentence, and I don't know whether it was because he realized the cops were listening, or because he suspected I really *was* that crazy.

Or maybe it's just that he didn't think I was listening, because I was hauling Dad out of the rear compartment. Dad was helping me as much as he could, but that wasn't much.

Grandfather Nakada's doctors were going to have some work to do getting my family back in shape, I thought. Assuming anyone bothered to do anything with Dad other than stick him back in a dreamtank.

The cab was settling down right next to the *Ukiba*—I mean, close enough that my feet wouldn't have to touch the plastic pavement at all, I'd step straight from the cab onto the metal steps. I heaved Dad onto my shoulder and got ready to jump, but paused long enough to com Perkins two words—"Open up." I knew the cops would intercept that, but I was hoping they might not realize I was talking to the ship rather than the cab, or that they simply wouldn't react quickly enough.

The cab opened up first, but only by a second or two; by the time I was solidly on the steps and trying to climb with my old man on my shoulder the airlock door was sliding aside.

I was relying on the fact that the cops were human, and had only human reaction times; the pause while they decided whether to shoot or not gave us time to get aboard the ship.

But only barely. Singh was right on my heels, with 'Chan on *his* shoulder, and the first trank bounced off the steps where his foot had been an instant before while I was still staggering into the airlock.

We made it, though, and the airlock closed up behind us, and the ship began moving the instant the outer door had a good seal.

If we'd been using a commercial vessel that would have been it, the authorities would have shut it down before it got off the ground, but I was pretty sure Yoshio Nakada wasn't the sort of person who would allow that. I'd gambled that the *Ukiba* did not have any of the standard police or port overrides—or at least, that they didn't actually override the ship's own systems.

The warning sirens were howling; we could hear them through the hull until we got through the inner door of the lock. I hoped the newsies and cops would all realize we meant it, and that the overrides weren't going to stop us; I didn't want anyone to be hurt by the launch.

I dumped Dad on the vibrating floor as soon as we were in the ship; he might only weigh half what he ought to, but that was still more than I was accustomed to carrying, and the ship's acceleration made any movement more difficult.

Singh lowered 'Chan to the deck, too, and we both sank down as well, and sat there leaning against the wall and panting as the roar of atmosphere past the hull peaked, and then began to fade.

"Mis' Hsing?" Perkins asked over the intercom.

"Right here," I said. "Everyone's aboard and alive."

"We're clear of the crater and heading for space," Perkins said. "I'm ignoring a lot of questions and demands from the ground."

I nodded, not that I thought he could see it. "Good."

"What's our destination?"

"American City," I told him. "The Nakada compound."

"Thank you. May I ask who our passengers are?"

I glanced around. "The one with the working legs is Minish Singh," I said. "He's a passenger—I promised him a ride off Epimetheus in exchange for his help with the others. The skin and bone near-corpse is my biological father, Guohan Hsing; we want to make sure he's healthy, then get him settled into a dreamery on Prometheus. And the last one's my brother Sebastian, who needs to have an implant removed before we can let him go."

"An implant? So we're being tracked?"

I sighed. "Perkins, we're staying in-system; they don't need an implant to track us."

"Oh. Of course not." There was a click; I didn't know whether he had really broken contact, but he seemed to be done talking.

"I assume you've got a surgeon lined up to take it out," 'Chan said.

"Not yet," I said. "We can take care of it when we get to Prometheus."

"Do you have a dream booked?" Dad asked.

"No." I saw the disapproving look on his face and said, "I'm improvising."

"You should have left me in the tank."

"Yes, I probably should," I agreed, "but I didn't trust Seventh Heaven to keep you alive in there once the Trap is in daylight."

"I hate this, Carlie," he said. "Everything hurts, and sometimes it's boring, and it seems dangerous. Someone could have shot at that cab, or at this ship."

"Run it," I said. "We should have you saved in a new tank in a couple of days."

"You know, you made a real mess back there," 'Chan said. "kidnapping and extortion and an unauthorized launch and probably a lot I don't know about. You better keep the Nakadas *really* happy; they're going to need to pay off a lot of people to clean that up."

"I intend to satisfy my client," I said.

'Chan heard the certainty in my voice. "So you think you know who killed Grandfather Nakada?"

I grimaced. "Nobody did," I said.

'Chan couldn't move his legs, but he threw up his hands at that. "Then what did they hire you for? If he died of natural causes, what do they need with a detective?"

"He didn't die," I said. I started to explain further, then stopped; it wasn't any of 'Chan's business.

"What, he faked his death? Why would he do that?"

I shook my head. "It's complicated," I said. "You don't need to know. All you need to know is that I got you out of Nightside City."

"With my legs locked up and my accounts probably frozen."

"We'll get that fixed. We'll get the implant out, and we'll get your money to Prometheus. You'll be fine."

"The Ginza is going to be furious if I don't go back."

"Screw the Ginza and IRC. We'll take care of it."

He stared at me. "You're running that smooth with the Nakadas?"

"I hope so." I looked at Singh. "You haven't been saying much."

He shrugged. "I don't have much to say. I wanted a ride off Epimetheus, and I'm getting one; I'm happy."

"A man of simple code," I said. "I like that."

"I may need some help with a breach of contract suit from Seventh Heaven."

"If they bother," I said.

"I said 'may.'"

I nodded.

Singh started to say something else, then took a look at my face and stopped; I guess he realized I wasn't listening any more.

I was thinking.

I was thinking about what Seventh Heaven might do about a stolen customer and poached employee, and that led me to the conclusion that it depended on the personalities involved, which led to me wondering exactly who the locals were who owned the Eta Cass franchise of Seventh Heaven, and that led me back to the back door into their systems, the back door that old Yoshio had had installed, but which someone else had recently been using.

Yoshio had the back door installed when he was thinking of acquiring the company, or at least the local division—I didn't know whether he'd been interested in the home office on Mars. Well, what if whoever had used the back door just before me had also been thinking about buying up the Eta Cass franchise of Seventh Heaven? With the dawn maybe a year away, the whole thing was probably available cheap.

In fact, maybe the original Yoshio had reconsidered and was taking another look. Yoshio-*kun* wouldn't know that, and the old man probably wouldn't have bothered mentioning it to me, since so far as he knew it was just another byte of business and had nothing to do with the tampering with his dream enhancer. Grandfather Nakada himself wasn't on Epimetheus and hadn't been lately, and I didn't think he could have used that back door over interplanetary distances; the delay in response time between Epimetheus and Prometheus was about eighteen minutes at the moment, and you couldn't sustain a connection with a break like that in it. He could have had one of his agents checking it out, though.

But if that was the case, then whoever used the back door hadn't needed the old man's ITEOD files to get access.

So maybe our little corporate explorer and the party who faked the old man's death weren't the same person at all; maybe it was just a coincidence, and the fraud had been after something else in the ITEOD files. Or maybe there was a connection I was missing.

Or maybe Yoshio had nothing to do with the intrusions, and I'd been right the first time. Or this was all part of some complicated corporate espionage that the old man might or might not know about.

I would have to ask him a few questions once we were safely back in American City.

But there were things I could check right here. "*Ukiba*," I said, "research request—I want to know the exact ownership of the local franchise of Seventh Heaven Neurosurgery, including any recent changes in ownership, or bids for purchase or control."

"Working," the ship replied. "How would you prefer the data to be presented?"

"Text display."

"Available."

We were clearing atmosphere by then, or at any rate the noise and vibration had subsided, so I was able to make my way to a terminal and look at what the ship had pulled off the nets—or maybe it had the information in its own files all along, for all I know; it might be something the old man liked to keep current.

As I suspected from its location, about thirty-four percent of Seventh Heaven Neurosurgery of Eta Cassiopeia was owned by IRC. Another eleven percent was owned by New Bechtel-Rand. The rest was spread across dozens of small investors, all based in the Eta Cass system, some in Nightside City, some on Prometheus.

And someone was trying to negotiate a takeover. An investment group calling itself Corporate Initiatives had approached IRC, New Bechtel-Rand, and several of the other shareholders with a tender offer—or rather, looking at the times, someone was approaching them right now.

I pulled up everything available on Corporate Initiatives. There wasn't much. Most of the listed contacts were software, the legal filings were all as vague as possible, the addresses were all just mail drops.

I knew there had to be a human agent listed somewhere, and eventually I found her. Her name was Chantilly Rhee, and at least legally, she was a resident of American City.

That was a surprise; I'd expected the whole thing to be based in Nightside City, or at least somewhere on Epimetheus. I asked for her background.

She was nine going on ten in Promethean years—twenty-six Epimethean, twenty-seven Terran. That was too young to be the real power here, I was pretty sure. Born in Muriel—that was a mining town on a caldera island just off the Nine Islands archipelago, a couple of hundred kilometers west of American City. That didn't tell me anything. Her parents weren't anyone special, a roomscape artist and a tactile therapist. Two younger sisters. Standard online education, got her checkmark when she was just five—sixteen Terran. Took half a year to travel, then found a job and settled in American City.

But then I saw what that job was, and Mis' Rhee got very interesting.

She was personal assistant to Kumiko Nakada—Yoshio Nakada's only surviving daughter.

Of course, Chantilly Rhee's involvement didn't mean that Yoshio's daughter was the one behind the assassination attempt; for one thing, if this was all connected and Kumiko was really the villain of the piece, I'd expect her to do a better job of hiding it. This could be coincidence, or misdirection, or one corner of a conspiracy.

Whatever it was, though, at least I finally had a suspect. When I got to American City I intended to have a chat with Grandfather Nakada, and then a little talk with his daughter. I doubted I would be able to get within twenty meters of her ordinarily, but with her father's backing I thought I ought to be able to arrange a conversation.

And one thing I wanted to know was what the hell she wanted with Seventh Heaven. Dream companies weren't exactly a hot item, last I heard; most people preferred real life. A dream company based in Nightside City seemed like an especially bad investment.

I remembered the case that got me off Epimetheus in the first place, when Sayuri Nakada had been conned into buying up worthless real estate by convincing her there was a way to keep the sun from rising and cooking Nightside City. What was it with Nakadas making stupid investments in a doomed city? Was Kumiko being conned, the way Sayuri was?

I knew it wasn't the same people; Sayuri was suckered by a group operating out of the Ipsy, the Institute for Planetological Studies of Epimetheus, and Grandfather Nakada had put a very definite stop to that. Those scammers were gone, sent for reconstruction.

But maybe they had friends. I frowned. Maybe the attempt on Grandfather Nakada had been an act of revenge, or maybe it had been intended to make sure he didn't do to these people what he did to Paulie Orchid, Bobo Rigmus, and Doc Lee. Maybe someone *was* running a con on Kumiko Nakada.

I wouldn't expect someone her age, in her position, to fall for any such scheme, but maybe they had a better pitch this time than the grit Sayuri bought into.

Or maybe it wasn't Kumiko after all; maybe Chantilly Rhee was the one being conned. She was young enough to be that dumb.

Or maybe she was part of the con, and Kumiko had bought in because she trusted Rhee.

And all that assumed there *was* a con, and this wasn't something completely different. I didn't actually know what was going on at all. It was even possible that Chantilly Rhee had been a front for Yoshio himself, and not Kumiko. I just didn't know.

But I intended to find out.

Chapter Fifteen

I called ahead, of course, to let Grandfather Nakada know we were coming. I didn't tell him exactly who "we" were, though—I don't care what encryption *Ukiba* used, I didn't think interplanetary communications could ever be secure. I didn't mention his daughter, or Seventh Heaven, or his own alleged death; I just said I was returning with passengers and needed to talk to him in person as soon as he could arrange it.

I got an acknowledgment that was even vaguer than my own message, saying that my situation would be discussed once we were on the ground.

I sent a follow-up, saying that some of our business was urgent. I didn't say what; I let him assume it was something to do with the murder attempt.

Really, though, it was Dad and 'Chan. Dad was starting to lose it, being out of his tank and no longer having his health monitored; the ship's medical banks could probably have handled him just fine if he'd allowed it, but he didn't trust me, or the ship, or anyone else, and said he would wait until we'd found him a new dreamtank. He insisted that the shaking hands and coughing fits and occasional spasms, and his inability to keep food down, were nothing to worry about.

And 'Chan was paralyzed from the waist down, which was more serious than I had initially thought. It wasn't just that he couldn't walk; there were other things he couldn't do, either. He was more cooperative than our father, so the ship was able to catheterize him, but still, I knew we needed to get that implant out as quickly as possible.

I thought about sending a message that we wanted a doctor standing by, but decided against it. Grandfather Nakada was two hundred and forty years old; it was a safe bet he *always* had doctors nearby, ready to work.

At least Singh was no problem. Now that we were actually on the way to Prometheus he seemed subdued and nervous, as if he was having second thoughts about his impulsive decision to get off Epimetheus. He'd left his belongings behind, and his friends, if he had any—he'd told me he didn't have any family, but not everyone we care about is related to us. I figured we'd be able to turn him loose with minimal fuss, maybe give him a few kilocredits to get started on his new life, and he'd be smooth, despite these belated doubts.

Yoshio-*kun* was another matter. I had no idea what I was going to do with him. I didn't know whether his existence was legal on Prometheus—I knew making a recording was illegal, but bringing in an already-existing one was another matter. The old man had done it more than once, but that didn't mean it was actually legal, and I wasn't him, and it might make a difference that Yoshio-*sempai* was still alive. I could have asked the ship, but I didn't actually care whether he was legal, only about whether I would need to hide his existence, and hiding him from his original was likely to be far more important than hiding him from the law. The old man might not want a copy of himself around, and not everyone thinks there's anything wrong in erasing artificial intelligences.

And it was the original Yoshio's ship. I was fairly sure the ship already knew Yoshio-*kun* existed, and Perkins definitely knew, but I didn't see any need to remind anyone by asking about the laws.

Of course, Yoshio-*kun* probably knew better than anyone else what Yoshio-*sempai* was likely to do, so I could have just asked him, but I was busy with Dad and 'Chan and I didn't get around to it.

Perkins put the ship down on the private Nakada field, where I was not happy to see daylight, and plenty of it; we were back in the realms of light. My feet felt heavier in Promethean gravity, as well, and the air that cycled in from outside smelled of ocean and volcanic smoke.

By the time I got through the airlock a dozen floaters were waiting for me, glittering in that horrible sunshine. "I have two people here who need medical attention," I told the nearest one the moment I emerged; I was shading my eyes with my hand and blinking, but I could see that it was a blue and silver floater that looked like the one I'd talked with in the Sakai building. It might have just been the same model, though.

"Yes, Mis' Hsing," it said. "They will be seen to immediately."

Floaters aren't exactly known for accurately simulating emotions such as surprise, but I still thought this one seemed to be prepared for my request. The ship had probably been in communication with the planetary networks before we landed.

"I expect you to be discreet," I said.

"We have strict instructions that everything about you and your activities is to be treated as confidential," it assured me.

"Good."

"You have an appointment with Yoshio Nakada in forty minutes. He trusts you will be prompt."

I stopped blinking and stared at the floater, my eyes starting to water. "Forty minutes?"

"Yes."

I had half expected him to be waiting on the landing field, but apparently he was in less of a hurry than I had thought. That meant I could oversee loading Dad and 'Chan into medical transports, and I could promise Dad that he would be going into a dreamtank as soon as we were sure he was healthy. Which wasn't necessarily true, since that hadn't been included in the agreement I made with the old man, but it kept everyone calm.

Singh was in the airlock when the medics left, staring out at the daylight. I realized he had probably never seen daylight first-hand before. We watched them go, and then Singh asked, "What about me?"

"Mis' Nakada would appreciate it if you would remain aboard the ship for the present," the blue-and-silver floater said.

"Am I being held?"

"Technically, you are trespassing, so the Nakadas would be within their rights to hold you. Mis' Nakada would prefer to keep this friendly, however."

"Friendly sounds good to me." Singh turned and headed back into the ship, probably looking for a snack, or hoping to talk Perkins into a game of something. I suspected he would just as soon wait until dark before venturing out into the thick, cool air of Prometheus.

And then it was time for me to head out to my appointment. Three floaters escorted me across the field and through a few corridors to a pleasant little office where daytime cloudscapes drifted across the walls, but where there were no actual windows.

The floaters waited at the door, and once I was inside the door snapped shut, locking them out and me in. I guessed the office was a secured area, and the floaters didn't have clearance to enter.

In fact, I was *sure* the office was a secured area; the old man would scarcely have talked to me anywhere else. At least we weren't meeting in a dressing room somewhere.

Yoshio Nakada was waiting for me, sitting comfortably in a big black chair that made him look small and old and harmless— probably deliberately. A small desktop floated by his right hand.

Nobody looks small to me, though, and I knew he wasn't harmless. I stepped in and stood there, waiting for him to speak first.

"Mis' Hsing," he said. "I see you have successfully collected your retainer."

"I have," I agreed. "Thank you. I trust their medical needs are being seen to, and my father will be installed in a dreamtank here?"

"They are. You don't mind, then, if Guohan Hsing is once again removed from your life?"

I shrugged. "That's what he wants. I respect my ancestor's wishes."

He nodded. "I expected nothing less. When you required his safety as part of your fee I assumed either familial duty or familial affection was basic to your character, and I thought duty more likely."

I didn't reply, and he continued, "You have left me with a mess to clean up, though—contracts broken, property stolen or destroyed, serious criminal charges."

"I know. I assume you can manage it."

"Of course I can. I would have preferred a tidier retrieval, though."

"I thought you were in a hurry."

"I am. Are you ready to begin your investigation, then?"

Since he knew something of what had happened on Epimetheus I had assumed he had kept himself informed about all of it, but maybe I'd misjudged, or maybe someone had been interfering, and he really didn't know all of what I'd done in Nightside City. "I already began it," I said.

That did not seem to surprise him any more than my agreeing to put my father back in a tank had. "Are you prepared to report any results?"

"I am prepared to discuss the situation, Mis' Nakada. I have questions I need answered."

"I will try to answer them, then." He gestured toward a chair, which floated up behind me. I settled into it.

"Did you know that everyone on Epimetheus thinks you're dead?" I asked.

He frowned. "You're sure?"

"Oh, very sure."

"I had hoped that the reports had been hacked."

I shook my head. "Not about that," I said. "Your death is all over the nets. Died in your sleep, cause undetermined. The newsies wanted to know what the hell I was doing with a dead man's ship."

"That must have been inconvenient."

"I managed."

"Do you know the origin of the false report of my death?"

"Here," I said, pointing at the floor. "Somewhere in American City, and someone with access to your private nets."

"You think it's related to the attempt on my life."

It wasn't a question, but I said, "Probably, yes. Are you negotiating the purchase of Seventh Heaven Neurosurgery?"

He tilted his head to one side. "I am not," he said.

"Someone here is. The buyer's human agent is Chantilly Rhee."

That appeared to surprise him—his eyes widened slightly. "I know Mis' Rhee," he said.

"So I assumed."

"I will not insult you by asking whether you are sure, but are you certain she is aware of her involvement?"

"No," I acknowledged. "Identity theft is definitely a possibility."

"Is this planned purchase related to the sabotage of my dream enhancer?"

"I don't know yet. It may be."

"The negotiations are taking place on Epimetheus?"

"I think so."

"Mis' Rhee has not left Prometheus since the attempt on my life. I have kept very careful track of everyone in the family compound."

"That assumes your surveillance software hasn't been compromised."

"True."

"I never said she was the buyer, though; she's listed as the agent, not the principal."

"You think my daughter is the principal?"

I noticed he took it for granted I knew who Chantilly Rhee worked for. "I don't know," I said. "Until this meeting, I wasn't sure *you* weren't the principal."

"While I am familiar with Seventh Heaven Neurosurgery, I decided some time ago that it was not a sound investment."

"I know," I said. "Poor long-term prospects. But you might have reconsidered."

"I haven't."

"*Someone* here thinks it's worth buying, though."

"Or worth appearing to want, at any rate."

"Or that."

"You seem to have learned some interesting things on Epimetheus, but I fail to see a connection to what I hired you to investigate."

"I don't know the link," I said. "Maybe there isn't one, but maybe there is. There's definitely a connection between Seventh Heaven and the false report of your death."

"Is there?"

"Yes. And that report scrolling past right after the attempt on your life would be one hell of a coincidence." I think he expected me to explain how the Seventh Heaven deal was related, but I didn't feel like explaining the business with the ITEOD files.

"You said the false report came from Prometheus."

"It did."

"But the negotiations with Seventh Heaven are being conducted on Epimetheus?"

"Oh, there's definitely been activity on both planets."

"Then if these events *are* connected, I am dealing with a conspiracy, and not a lone assassin."

"Well, it's not a single individual, acting entirely alone," I agreed. "But your assassin might just have hired help. Or bought it."

"Ah. Software might be conducting the negotiations with Seventh Heaven."

"Yes. And software might have made the phony death report."

"Interesting."

"Do you have any idea why anyone would want to buy Seventh Heaven?"

"Just the local franchise, or the parent company?"

"The local franchise. I don't care about anything on Mars, or anywhere else outside our system."

He shook his head. "Their prospects are not good. The resident population of Nightside City is less than half what it was before the first light topped the crater wall, and those who remain are more likely to invest in a ticket off-planet than in a dream company's services. They have failed to establish themselves anywhere else in the Eta Cass system, not even elsewhere on Epimetheus; the franchise operators don't seem to have considered it worth investing the necessary capital, and the costs to start now would be prohibitive. Seventh Heaven's present business model has no future, and I am unaware of any plans to refocus their resources."

"Oh, I know no one's stupid enough to want them as they are now," I said. "I was thinking about whether they have anything that could be valuable in some completely different way. Their dream library, maybe?"

"Their library is unremarkable," the old man said.

I didn't bother asking how he could be sure, or what standards he used to evaluate it; I didn't doubt he knew what he was talking about. Instead I asked, "What else do they have?"

"You believe this is relevant?"

"It might be. I don't know. If I can show that it isn't, that's one less dead link to explore."

He considered for a moment, then said, "Their assets consist of the tanks, which have no obvious use other than their present one; the trust fund that is intended to fund maintenance until their last client dies; the dream library; a diminished sales staff; long-term leases on property in Trap Under; and their client contracts. The sales staff and library are completely unremarkable."

"That trust fund—is that worth chasing?"

"Not unless they intend to murder all their clients."

I felt a chill at that, and Grandfather Nakada must have read it on my face. "That isn't a viable option," he said. "While it's true that their client base has little connection to the outside world, all deaths are reported to the city authorities—by the tanks, not by the personnel—and any suspicious increase in mortality would be noticed."

"You're assuming they don't hack the tanks to prevent the death reports."

"Mis' Hsing, if the deaths aren't reported, the trust fund won't be released."

"Could they bribe the city authorities to ignore suspicions?"

"Of course they could, but corruption always carries some risk, and the amount in the trust fund would not justify that risk—it would barely cover the bribes. What's more, some of the clients left family behind who would not be so easily silenced."

I had to admit that it didn't sound like a good reason to buy the company. I wondered where those black floaters that had helped me get my father out fit in; did the buyers *want* the clients to be removed? Would that free up the trust fund?

But they couldn't count on clients to have crazy relatives. That wasn't it.

From Yoshio's list, that left the leases and the contracts.

"Is space in Trap Under at a premium, maybe?" I asked. "Do people think it'll be protected from the sun?"

"It *will* be protected from the sun," the old man answered, "but no, it isn't particularly valuable. There's more than enough space available, and new tunnels can be bored cheaply enough. The city's economy is based on a liveable external environment; if it has to move underground it won't be any different than any of the mining towns further out on the night side, except that there's nothing worth mining. The tourist trade will disappear, and most of the miners will make do with their own casinos and entertainments."

That left the contracts.

The old man came to the same conclusion, and before I could ask a question he said, "The client contracts are more of a liability than an asset. The money has already been paid in, and what's left is the obligation to care for and entertain the clients."

I knew he was right, but I thought there was something there we were missing. Those black floaters—*had* they deliberately been helping me get Dad out of there? They didn't belong to Seventh Heaven or the Ginza; they belonged to the New York, which meant the Nakadas, which probably meant whoever was backing Corporate Initiatives. The buyers had helped me kidnap one of the clients—what did that mean?

Did they want Dad out of his tank? If so, why? What did a Nakada want with him?

Whatever it was, I had brought him straight to the Nakada family's private compound.

"Where's my father?" I asked.

"Medical services, I assume."

"Could you check?"

If I had to describe Nakada's expression I would call it "bemused." He didn't say anything; he turned to his desktop and pressed a thumb on a reader.

The seascape that had filled the display vanished, and menus appeared. He gestured, then read the results.

"He's in medical services, undergoing an examination."

"Who has access to the exam results?"

The old man's expression changed, so slightly I wasn't entirely sure at first I hadn't imagined it. "That's a very interesting question," he replied. He reached up to the back of his neck, and I realized for the first time that he was jacked in, and the desktop was for my benefit, not his. He'd found my question interesting enough to drop the grit.

I wouldn't have thought he'd want to ride wire after what happened to his dream enhancer, but apparently he wasn't deterred as easily as I was. I assume he had massive security on that line, the sort of watchdogs I had only ever seen from the outside.

"You're right, Mis' Hsing," he said, though I hadn't said anything to be right about. "Someone's hacked into medical and taken a very sharp interest in your father's condition."

"Can you tell who?"

"I can limit the possibilities," he said. "There are about a dozen."

"Is Chantilly Rhee one of them?"

"Yes. So is Kumiko."

"I'd guess some of the others are dead."

His eyes had drifted off, upward and to the right, since I asked who had access, but now they snapped back and focused directly on mine. "Oh?"

"I know there are at least eight uploads of dead Nakadas running in this compound, and I'd be surprised if none of them could get in there if they wanted to."

"I am impressed, Mis' Hsing. I am quite sure I did not mention my uploaded siblings and descendants to you."

"I told you I'd started my investigation."

"I will want to know more about this eventually, but for now, let us keep our attention on more urgent matters. You tell me that my daughter's aide is involved in a scheme to purchase Seventh Heaven Neurosurgery, a company that is, by any rational standard, almost worthless. You seem convinced this is linked to the attempt on my life. And I believe we have both concluded that what the buyers are actually after is not any of the company's normal assets, but the people inside the dreamtanks."

"I think they helped me get my father out of there," I said. I didn't bother telling him any details about the black floaters; they weren't relevant.

"You think they wanted him to serve as a test sample, so they could assess the condition of their intended acquisitions. Helping you kidnap him was less likely to draw unwelcome attention than extracting one of the dreamers themselves."

The old man was still sharp. "Yes," I said.

"It's an interesting theory, Mis' Hsing, but it's based on very little evidence and a great deal of supposition. Further, there is one very basic question to which I do not see an obvious answer: What do they *want* with the dreamers?"

When I walked into the office I couldn't have answered that question, but by this time I had figured it out.

"Bodies," I said. "They want living bodies that their original owners aren't using."

Chapter Sixteen

For a moment Grandfather Nakada sat silently in his big chair, staring at me. Then he said, "You think one of my uploaded relatives wants to be human again?"

"At *least* one," I said. "For all I know, all eight of them are conspiring in this."

"I confess, Mis' Hsing, I don't even know whether it's technically possible to download a mind from a network into a human body."

"I don't, either. And I wouldn't be too sure *they* know. That doesn't mean they won't try it. If they buy up Seventh Heaven they'll have plenty of bodies to experiment on, and if they wait until after sunrise there won't be much of anyone left in Nightside City to notice or care."

The old man considered that for a few seconds, then said, "Very little evidence and a great deal of supposition, Mis' Hsing. And it doesn't explain the attempt on my life, or the false reports of my death."

"They wanted a copy of you," I said. "To get them into Seventh Heaven. They didn't think you'd cooperate with them in your present form, but if you died, and an upload of you was booted up, they thought the upload would help them. In fact, it apparently has —when you survived the assassination attempt, they realized a false report of your death would release the ITEOD files, and they could copy and activate the upload you had in there."

"They have a copy of me?" The old man looked shocked. I hadn't thought anything could shock someone who'd lived through the last two centuries, but it seemed I was wrong. I suppose this was a bit more personal than all that history.

And while I hadn't originally intended to bring this up, I wanted to see how he would react to another news item.

"So do I," I said. "Aboard *Ukiba*."

"Hsing, you..."

He stopped in mid-sentence, staring at me, speechless.

I felt a twinge of guilt about popping that up on the old man. I didn't want to kill off my client, after all, and at his age any sort of shock carried a risk. "I didn't know who it was," I said. "If there's a proper catalog in the ITEOD files, I missed it."

He stared at me for a moment, then said, "So you think—you think that someone in my own family tried to *kill* me, just to get control of a copy of my most recent upload, as part of this scheme to use dreamers as a source of new bodies?"

"Yes, I do," I said, "if you consider uploads to still be family members. Remember, to an upload, that copy may be *you*. She wouldn't really be killing you at all, just switching you to her own form of life, and even that might only be temporary."

"An incarnationist? You think one of my uploaded relatives is an incarnationist?"

I hadn't heard the term "incarnationist" before, but I understood right away what it meant, and what the tone of voice Nakada was using meant, as well. I had never seen the old man so flustered—in fact, until now I had never seen him flustered at all. Now, though, he seemed thoroughly scrambled. He clearly found the idea that a member of his own family could believe in the transferability of identity repulsive.

"There might be other motives as well," I said.

"And there are *two* active copies of me?"

"I don't know whether theirs is still active," I said. A thought struck me at the mention of the copies. "I'll bet that...well, I didn't find any record of any human suspects visiting Epimetheus lately, but I'll bet one of your uploads transmitted a copy there, and that's who's been running the Seventh Heaven negotiations."

"You think there's a duplicate of one of *them*, too?"

"And you can probably find out which by checking transmission records."

He blinked, and his jaw sagged slightly, and I remembered that he was still jacked in. I could guess where in the nets he was going.

Then he was back, his face hardening. "Shinichiro," he said. "My son Shinichiro."

I knew the name from the family records; his was the most recent of the three deaths among the old man's children, and he had been dead for about twenty Terran years. I didn't know much beyond that, so I didn't say anything.

"A copy was transmitted, just as you said."

"Then I think he's your assassin," I said. "Or at least the ringleader."

"But you have no proof."

"I have no proof," I agreed.

"Then you have not completed the job to my satisfaction."

"I've identified the assassin."

"You've named a likely suspect. That's not good enough. To accuse my own son, I need more than this web of suppositions and guesswork."

"It's not your son," I said. "It's an upload that thinks it's your son."

The old man's face froze at that, and then took on a new expression.

I don't ever want to see anyone look at me like that again. Usually the old man hid his emotions, kept everything under strict control, but I'd cracked that reserve earlier, and right then it broke completely. Despair and rage were written in his eyes and on every feature.

Maybe it was an act. Maybe he was really still as cold and controlled as ever, and pasted that look there deliberately.

I don't think so, though. I think I had touched something he really cared about, said something he didn't want to hear—and something that he knew was true.

"I talked to the copy of you aboard *Ukiba*," I said. "It knew what it was. It knew it wasn't you. It knew an upload isn't human, no matter what it's copied from, and that means *you* know it. You *know* that's the truth. That upload isn't your son; it's an imitation, a software emulation."

"It's all I have left of him," the old man said.

"But it's not *him*," I insisted. "It's software, not wetware."

"It's all that's left," he repeated, "and if you're going to accuse him of trying to murder me, I need more proof than you've given me so far."

I wasn't really surprised. He had told me he thought it was a member of the family, and he had seemed to accept the idea, but that was when it was theoretical and non-specific. Now that it was a particular individual, one who he apparently loved, it was different.

"I need access to your family networks, then," I said. "And I'd like to interview Chantilly Rhee, and Kumiko Nakada, and the upload you call Shinichiro, in that order."

"I'll arrange it." His voice was cold again.

Something about the way he said it beeped for me. "You *know* Shinichiro did it," I said. "You just want proof."

"I believe that's what I said, Mis' Hsing."

He had obviously recovered from his moment of shock.

"Fine. I'll get you your proof. Maybe not enough for the law, but enough for you to be sure."

"That is all I ask."

"How soon can I see Mis' Rhee?"

"I believe she should be at her desk; would you prefer to speak to her in private?"

"I'd prefer to speak to her somewhere I know the Shinichiro upload isn't listening."

Even as I said it, though, I realized it was probably too late to keep it from learning what was going on. While I was sure the old man had a dozen layers of security on the office we were in, Yoshio-*sempai* had checked on the medicals and on the transmission logs, and there were probably a dozen other beeps as well—the upload might not know we had narrowed it down to a single entity, but it must know we were getting close. It had already tried to kill the old man once, and just as I said, it wouldn't even see it as murder—as far as Shinichiro was concerned his father was safely backed up in a couple of places, and shutting down his original meatware was just a maintenance issue; he'd be rebooted as soon as possible.

As for me, I wasn't family, I wasn't important, I wasn't anyone. Killing me was just debugging the situation. If I was lucky it might try to buy me off instead, but if it really had access to a running copy of the Yoshio upload a simple question would tell it that wasn't going to work.

At least, I certainly hoped the old man's back-up would have that much respect for me; Grandfather Nakada had certainly claimed to when he hired me.

That brought up an interesting question, though—*was* Shinichiro's copy of Yoshio-*kun* cooperating? Did it agree with what Shinichiro was trying to do? From what I knew of the old man's character, I didn't think it would, but it might play along until it had control of its situation.

It didn't really matter, though; that copy of Yoshio-*kun* was back on Epimetheus, and I was here in the Nakada compound in American City.

A lot of things were fitting together. It must have been a copy of Shinichiro that sent those black floaters after me in the Trap; the copy here on Prometheus probably had floaters, too. It must have access to a *lot* of things. I didn't know how much control it might have over the household's environment—could it override the normal protocols? It had gotten at the old man's dream enhancer, so it had obviously hacked at least some of the systems beyond what it was supposed to be capable of using. There was no way to be sure *anywhere* in American City was entirely safe—or anywhere on the entire planet, really. This office *might* be secure, but if the old man had been assuming a human saboteur he might have missed a way in. Ordinarily software was written so that it couldn't harm people and didn't *want* to, but uploads—well, that was part of why they were illegal most places. Uploads could do things artificials couldn't, could go places humans couldn't. They didn't need to eat or sleep, and could be invisible and silent. Most of them didn't go hacking into secure systems, but if they wanted to, they'd be hard to stop.

If Grandfather Nakada got through this alive, he was going to need to run some serious purges.

For now, though, I was supposed to be interviewing suspects, to demonstrate to the old man that Shinichiro was responsible for the attempted murder.

"Could we talk in here?" I suggested. This room was probably as safe as I was going to get. "I don't think I'd be comfortable questioning her in her own office."

"Would you prefer me to be present or absent?"

"I don't think it matters. You'll be recording it, I'm sure."

"Of course."

"Then it doesn't matter."

He nodded. "I've notified her to come immediately."

I nodded, and settled back in my chair to wait. The old man turned to his desktop and started working on something, ignoring me for the moment.

It was a good chair, very comfortable, and the cloudscapes on the walls were soothing. I found myself starting to relax.

"Mis' Hsing," Yoshio said, startling me back to full alertness.

"Yeah?"

"I thought you would like to know that your brother has come through surgery well; the implant has been removed, and I have convinced IRC to accept a payment in lieu of his services. Do you know whether he has any employment prospects on Prometheus?"

"I don't," I said.

"He may find breaking his contract with IRC will make him less appealing to potential employers."

I shrugged. "He's a grown man. He'll manage."

"Considering the effort you devoted to getting him out of Nightside City, you seem surprisingly unconcerned."

"He's my brother, so I care about him, but he's not a baby."

"I have arranged for Guohan Hsing to be tanked at Eternal Adventures here in American City as soon as his condition is sufficiently stable; my medical systems estimate forty hours will be more than adequate. Obtaining his personal library from Seventh Heaven may prove difficult, however. They have accepted my payment for breach of contract and damages, but seem determined to hold his accumulated dream experiences for ransom."

"Then he can start a new library."

"You aren't concerned?"

"I think I've fulfilled my filial responsibilities, thank you."

"Forgive me for saying so, but you don't seem very fond of your family."

"My father dumped his three kids to buy a dream; do you expect me to be grateful?"

"And your brother?"

I hesitated. "I love 'Chan," I said. "I really do. But... do you love your niece Narumi?"

He smiled. "I understand. Moving on, this man Singh—who is he?"

"He's a maintenance worker from Seventh Heaven who agreed to help me in exchange for a ride to Prometheus. End of script. I got him here, contract's complete."

"You don't believe him to be involved in the alleged conspiracy?"

I shook my head. "If he is, he is one fine, fine actor."

"Is he aware that I hired you?"

I had to think about that. I hadn't actually told him, but he could have asked Perkins, or *Ukiba*...

"I don't know," I said.

"In your opinion, is he likely to object to a partial memory erasure?"

It seemed the old man was already thinking about the clean up. "I don't know," I repeated. "I think it would depend on the terms."

"And your brother?"

"My *brother*," I said, "agreed to that implant IRC put in him. I don't think he'd mind a little mental meddling if there was some sort of compensation."

"Compensation can be arranged."

"Then he's all yours. And Dad won't say anything while he's in a tank, so even if he knew anything you wouldn't need to worry."

Yoshio nodded. "And you?"

"No."

"No?"

"No one meddles with my memory if I have anything to say about it. Personal integrity aside, I can't afford the risk in my line of work—what if you erased knowledge of an enemy I need to defend against?" I shook my head. "No."

"I am not surprised."

"I didn't think you would be."

"Nonetheless, I thought it worth asking."

I shrugged. Then I sat up and looked around. The door hadn't moved; the cloudscapes still drifted undisturbed across the walls. "When will Rhee be here?"

The old man frowned. He glanced at the desktop, then put a hand up to the back of his neck to adjust the connection. "I've lost track of her," he said.

"What?"

"Her location is not registering."

I reached down to where my gun would have been if I'd been allowed to bring it. I hadn't been, of course; I'd barely bothered to ask. "Are there dead areas close to this office?"

"No."

"She's making a run for it?"

"Possibly. There are other explanations."

"She might have been intercepted, you mean? Or your instructions never reached her, or were countermanded?"

"You grasp the situation well."

"So Shinichiro *does*..." I saw the old man's mouth tighten, and corrected myself. "It would appear that whoever is behind this is aware that we're getting close."

"So it would seem," Yoshio agreed.

"I need to go after her, then." I got out of the chair. "Can you direct me to her last known location?"

"I can have a floater guide you..." he began.

But then he stopped and looked surprised.

I had been starting toward the door, but looking back over my shoulder toward the old man, so I saw his face, saw his eyes widen. I stopped moving, and turned to look where he was looking.

That wasn't necessarily going to let me see whatever he was seeing, since he was still jacked in, but it's an instinctive thing, probably goes back a million years. I found myself looking at the door to the corridor.

I didn't see anything strange, just a closed door, so I started walking again.

The door didn't open. I was almost close enough to touch it, and it didn't budge.

"I've been overridden," Grandfather Nakada said from behind me.

"Overridden how?" I asked, turning back.

"I can't open the door," he replied.

"I thought this office was secure."

"So did I."

That was really not what I wanted to hear just then. "How badly are we screwed?" I asked.

He didn't try to smooth it. "I'm not sure," he said. "I cannot say how badly compromised the data I'm receiving is." He pulled the plug from his neck and let it retract, then turned to the desktop.

I didn't wait; I ran my hand down the wall, through the images of fluffy white clouds, and found the manual emergency release. I twisted the handle, and the door cranked open a few centimeters.

I saw motion in the passageway outside, and stopped. I peered through the crack.

The blue-and-silver floater was there, hovering directly in front of the crack but turned to face away from us.

Beyond it were at least two other floaters, sleek black ones, that seemed to be keeping the blue one pinned in place.

"Father," an unfamiliar voice said.

I turned. The desktop had lit up with a face—a face I didn't recognize, and one that wasn't exactly 100% human.

"Shinichiro," the old man said.

"Father," the desktop repeated. "We need to talk."

Chapter Seventeen

"I am listening," Yoshio said.

"I believe that this woman Hsing may have misled you." The face on the desktop moved as if speaking, but was very slightly out of sync with the words we heard. I guessed that the upload only had limited bandwidth to work with; presumably Grandfather Nakada had strictly controlled access to the device.

The old man threw me a quick glance. "In what way?"

"I suspect she may have cast a false light upon my situation in hopes of coaxing money and perhaps other concessions from you."

"What situation is that, Shinichiro?"

"There is an experiment I hope to conduct, and I have been pursuing the means to perform it. This involves purchasing a controlling interest in Seventh Heaven Neurosurgery. Since I am at present inconvenienced by my physical nature, I have been forced to make this purchase secretly, through intermediaries."

"You refer to the legal insistence that software cannot own stock, or control corporations."

"Yes, Father."

"What does this have to do with Carlisle Hsing?"

"It appears, Father, that Mis' Hsing has learned of my intentions—I do not know how, but she is, as we know, a talented and experienced investigator. I believe she has misinterpreted my plans. She kidnapped Guohan Hsing from Seventh Heaven, and I assume she did so because she thought his life might be in danger. I take it she has come here to tell you of her misapprehensions, and ask that I be prevented from continuing my activities."

"Her business with me is not your concern."

"As you please, Father. But I want to assure you, I do not intend to harm anyone."

The old man looked at me questioningly; I looked back blankly and shrugged slightly. I had no idea where this was going.

"I note that you have interfered with the household systems," Yoshio said.

"Only so that I might defend myself from slander, Father!"

"Go on, then. What is this experiment? What do you want with Seventh Heaven Neurosurgery? You know I declined to purchase it some time ago; what makes it worth your while now?"

"The contract terms for the clients, Father. They granted Seventh Heaven a great deal of control over their physical well-being, and as I read the terms, this allows Seventh Heaven to make arrangements that would not be legal under other circumstances."

"Let us dispense with pretense and delay, Shinichiro," the old man said wearily. "What is this experiment you want to attempt? What do you hope to do with Seventh Heaven's clients? Explain it to me."

The tone of the voice from the desktop changed, from formally polite to forceful and direct. "These people have human bodies they aren't using, Father, while I, and other uploaded personalities, would very much like to be human again—the legal restrictions on us are surprisingly onerous. I want to be able to own property and conduct business without a slew of artificial constraints. I want to be able to go places that aren't on the open nets or the family's systems. I want to have a discrete body again. I can't just grow myself one; you know about that. If it has a functioning brain, then it's a person in its own right, and I can't download myself into it without being charged with murder. If it doesn't have a functioning brain, there's no way to download me into it at all. But these people, Father, have brains and bodies they're barely using, and have signed away half their rights to the company. As I read the contracts, I think it would be legal to remove them from their bodies completely, and put us—myself and other uploads—in those bodies instead."

"*Remove* them?" Yoshio asked.

"Upload them," the desktop said eagerly. "Just the way you uploaded me. They've signed away so much control that I believe Seventh Heaven can legally remove them from their bodies entirely."

"Against their will?"

"No, no, of course not! We would *ask* them, and offer them a choice—stay in the dreamtanks until they die of old age or systems failure, or transfer to electronic form where they can live forever, where they can, if they want, be removed from Epimetheus entirely so that they don't need to worry about what will happen if Nightside City is abandoned and left derelict. And they can go right on dreaming—we would transfer their dream libraries with them, and set those up in the same nets that their minds would be in. They wouldn't need to interact with the outside world at all, any more than they do now; they could have dedicated systems. They could exist in their imaginary worlds, in realms of light, worlds of bliss, untroubled by any lingering concerns about their original flesh."

My skin crawled slightly at that idea; these disembodied intelligences would be so isolated, so *pointless*.

I didn't say anything, though; this was between the two of them.

"But they would be dead," Yoshio said.

"What? No, they would be just as alive as I am, living electronically, and their bodies would be inhabited by me, and Shigeru, and Momoko, and Hideo, and Kazuo—and *you*, if you want. You could be younger, Father—you're two hundred years old, and even the best doctors can't keep you alive as you are forever, but you could start over in a younger body, one the original owner doesn't want anymore."

"Shinichiro..." The old man looked desperately unhappy; he stared at me for a second before saying, "No. Shinichiro is dead. You are a recording. You are not my son."

"Father, what are you saying?" The desktop's tone was quite convincingly shocked. "I *am* Shinichiro!"

"You are a piece of software that *thinks* it's my son. And if you were downloaded into a new body, even one cloned from your own genes, you would *still* not be my son. My son is dead. You would only be a copy."

"But Father, what difference does that make?" The desktop's voice was baffled and angry—and, I thought, frightened. "I'm still *me*. A copy is as good as the original."

Yoshio shook his head. "If I scan something, the copy may be indistinguishable from the original, but it is not the original."

"But there's no difference! I remember everything, and what makes us who we are, but our memories? I remember growing up with Kumiko and Shigeru, and you came to see us every night and put us to bed, and I made you tuck in my bunny—how can I remember that if I'm not your son?"

Yoshio did not answer immediately; he sat in his big black chair, staring at me, with the desktop floating by his shoulder.

"Father, I *am* Shinichiro, and I want to be human again. I want my rights back." It sounded desperate. "Your shielding worked, so I don't know what Hsing has told you, and I don't know how she found out something was going on with Seventh Heaven, but I promise you, I don't mean anyone any harm. I just want to be human again, and I couldn't think of any other way to do it. It's her fault I even thought of *this* one—I got the idea when I did a background check on her for you, when she found out what Sayuri was doing. I found out where her father was, and that it was the same company you had looked at, and I realized that there were all those bodies going unused, zipped up in Nightside City where no one would ever notice if they were recycled. I wasn't going to steal them; I would ask for volunteers, and trade eternal life for humanity. I wasn't doing anything terrible. I wasn't going to hurt Guohan Hsing."

"You hacked his medical exam."

"It was a perfect chance to see just what condition the dreamers are in!"

"You faked my death."

"I... no, *I* didn't." I had never heard an electronic intelligence hesitate like that before; it was the most human thing the Shinichiro upload had done in the entire conversation.

"A copy of you did," the old man said.

Something here didn't yet fit, I realized. If Shinichiro had been the power behind Corporate Initiatives, which intended to buy Seventh Heaven, why had it used the back door to explore the company files? Why not just wait until it had legal control? It had just said that it knew the old man had looked at Seventh Heaven, so it did know the back door was there and that a Yoshio-*kun* could get it in, but why bother? Why was it worth faking Grandfather's death?

Why bother hacking my father's exam, instead of just demanding medical data as a condition of the planned purchase?

And why had it been our attempt to talk to Chantilly Rhee that forced the upload to hack in and talk to the old man?

The upload talked about wanting human rights. It hadn't said a thing about wanting a body for its own sake; it hadn't mentioned wanting to *feel* human again. It hadn't said anything about food or sex or physical sensations of any kind, and those were the things that the other uploads I'd talked to or heard about associated with being human, the things they thought they had lost. Shinichiro had been dead for twenty years; it might not even *remember* those. Yes, it remembered the bedtime bunny, but did it remember lust or pain or hunger? It hadn't mentioned them.

It had talked about the right to own stock, instead. But what did it want to own? Seventh Heaven was just a means to an end, not the ultimate goal—buying Seventh Heaven in order to be able to buy Seventh Heaven didn't make any sense, so there had to be more.

And it had apparently tried to murder the old man *first*, before it started hacking into Seventh Heaven.

It didn't want Seventh Heaven; it wanted Nakada Enterprises. I was sure of it. When I first heard that someone had tried to kill Grandfather Nakada, and that he suspected his own family, that was the obvious motive.

But an upload couldn't inherit anything; it wasn't human.

If Shinichiro had been behind the entire thing, you might think he wouldn't have wanted the old man dead until *after* he was human again, and able to inherit—but that assumed that Yoshio would have named the new Shinichiro as his heir, and I knew he wouldn't have. The upload must have known it, too. There was no legal link between Grandfather Nakada and some dreamer's corpse with a new personality imprinted on it; any inheritance would need to be set up by Yoshio himself, and he wouldn't have done it.

But someone else might have. Someone might have agreed to help take over Seventh Heaven, and help put Shinichiro into a new body, and even share control of Nakada Enterprises, in exchange for disposing of Yoshio.

And that someone might have changed her mind when the first attempt failed. She might have lost her nerve, or decided that Shinichiro wasn't as competent as she had thought.

And then the Shinichiro upload would have had to act on its own, trying to get control of Seventh Heaven, or maybe just get enough data to convince its co-conspirator to come back on screen.

If I was right about this, then copying itself to Epimetheus, faking the old man's death, and breaking into Seventh Heaven had all been a back-up plan, something it did because the assassination failed and its partner backed out.

I had looked at Grandfather Nakada's will, of course. It was a complicated thing, befitting the patriarch of one of the great corporate clans, but it had also been very traditional in some regards, and one of those was that it left control of Nakada Enterprises, along with holdings worth billions of credits, to the old man's surviving children.

Three of his five children were dead. The survivors were Kumiko and Hideo, and Chantilly Rhee worked for Kumiko.

She must have been in on it all initially, but dropped out and left Shinichiro on its own. *Then* everything fit. The upload must have diverted Rhee out of fear that she would tell the old man of Kumiko's involvement, and Kumiko would try to clear her own name by incriminating her uploaded brother. By popping up with its own version of events the upload was forestalling that—or trying to.

It occurred to me that maybe Kumiko had dropped out not because of any doubts, but because she simply didn't have the money to buy Seventh Heaven without that inheritance. A little check into Kumiko's financial situation might be in order once we were out of this room and the old man was back in control of the household systems.

"It was a mistake, Father," the upload said. "I am most heartily sorry for it."

I thought the old man was going to ask whether hacking the dream enhancer was a mistake, too, but he didn't.

"We will need to issue a correction," he said.

"Of course," the upload agreed.

"You will need to release control of the household systems."

"In due time, Father, but I'm sure you'll understand if I wait until I'm certain we have reached agreement about my future."

The old man frowned. "I suppose that's acceptable for now."

The door behind me suddenly slid fully open, and the black floaters backed away. "I regret holding you this way until we could talk," the desktop said. "Now that we understand the situation better, though, perhaps it's time for Mis' Hsing to go."

I certainly understood the situation; the upload wanted me out of the way so it could kill Yoshio.

It hadn't killed him while I was on Epimetheus because he was on guard, and besides, it didn't want to give Kumiko everything she wanted without some assurance that she would hold up her end of their bargain. It had been keeping its options open. Now that it had been beeped, though, and the old man knew who was responsible, the risk of leaving him alive was too great.

Killing him while I was there, though, meant it would need to kill me, too, which was too suspicious. If it could get me to leave, then it could go ahead and dispose of the old man, and take care of me later. I didn't know whether it might try to bribe or blackmail me, or whether it would go straight to assassination, but I knew that it would want me out of the way, and my life expectancy would plummet.

That was how I read the situation, anyway. Oh, it was pretending to believe that kindly old Grandfather Nakada was willing to make peace, to forgive its little peccadilloes, but I wasn't buying it. Shinichiro knew his father, surely, and knew what the old man was capable of, how hard he could be. It had been willing to kill him before, when he had been completely unsuspecting, so why would it hesitate now? To the upload, after all, it wasn't really death

—Yoshio was backed up on several coms. Losing his human body wasn't the end, merely a temporary inconvenience, and that body couldn't last much longer anyway.

The old man, of course, saw it differently, and had no intention of dying any time soon. He was playing along with the upload, but I knew he didn't believe it—he hadn't asked about the dream enhancer, or about a dozen other things that he would have wanted explained if he really thought the upload was sincere.

I was pretty sure he knew it intended to kill him, too.

"Perhaps, Mis' Hsing, I might have *Ukiba* fly you back to Alderstadt?" he said.

"I'd appreciate that," I said. "My stuff is aboard the ship; I can pack it up on the way."

"I will accompany you to the ship, then," the old man said, getting to his feet. "I have a few matters to discuss with Captain Perkins, in any case."

"I can provide a link," the desktop said.

"I think I prefer to speak to him in person," Yoshio insisted.

"Honestly, Father, I won't interfere with the connection. I won't even listen in."

"Thank you, Shinichiro, but the exercise will do me good." He waved to me, and to the blue-and-silver floater. "This way."

I knew the way; I don't need a guide for a route I've followed once. I didn't say that, of course. I let the old man take the lead as we made our way back out to the landing field.

Shinichiro let us go; a direct attack would be too obvious, and he didn't know what defenses we might have. The floaters made no move to stop us, or interfere at all as we walked back out to the field together.

I barely knew what to expect when we emerged into the open air and that ghastly sunlight, but everything was much as I'd left it.

The field was mostly deserted. The ship was still there, and the airlock's outer door was open.

I didn't think Shinichiro had compromised the ship's systems. I thought that if we could get aboard, we might get away. I'd already made one illegal hot launch; another wouldn't bother me.

I hadn't dared call ahead, though; Shinichiro was almost certainly listening. The drive wouldn't be run up. We'd need a few minutes to get *Ukiba* spaceworthy.

There was also the issue of where we would land. The two copies of Shinichiro had probably infiltrated systems all over Prometheus and Epimetheus, not just in Nightside City and American City. That fake death report had been completely convincing; it hadn't tripped any scam filters *anywhere*. That might mean Shinichiro had done a perfect job generating it and just got lucky that no one wanted more details and was willing to dig for them, or it might mean that it had subverted all the systems that might have tried to verify the story. The latter seemed more likely.

So the two inhabited planets were compromised, and Cass II wouldn't work; we didn't have the equipment to survive on the molten surface, and the pitiful little colony there wouldn't have any room to spare for us, or anywhere we could hide. Cass I wasn't even as viable as Cass II—it was a tiny, airless ball of radioactive slag that barely qualified as a planet, too close to Eta Cass A to be any use to anyone. If we couldn't find a friendly port on Epimetheus or Prometheus, we'd need to leave the Eta Cassiopeia system entirely. *Ukiba* did have a full Wheeler drive, but I didn't know whether it was ready for interstellar flight.

I didn't know whether *I* was ready for interstellar flight, either; I'd never given it any serious thought. I never had a reason to.

I didn't know how long it would take to reach an inhabited system; I didn't know *Ukiba*'s specs. The possibility of spending half a year with the old man and Perkins and Singh, not to mention

Yoshio-*kun*, was not appealing, but it might be the only way for Grandfather Nakada and me to survive.

Whether the old man could ever regain control of Nakada Enterprises was another program entirely, and one I wasn't going to worry about yet. I had enough grit to deal with.

At least Dad and 'Chan were off the ship.

I realized I didn't know whether Singh and Perkins were still aboard or not. If Perkins had gone off duty, this might get complicated.

I smiled wryly at the thought. It already *was* complicated; Perkins' absence would just make it more so. But the old man had said he was coming out here to talk to Perkins, so the roundeye was presumably still on the ship.

The old man's blue-and-silver floater had followed us, and an entire swarm of other floaters had collected as well; I didn't think any of those others were on our side.

We climbed the ramp with floaters all around us; in fact, a couple of small ones followed us right into the airlock. Apparently Shinichiro was not about to leave his father unattended.

We both saw them, but didn't say anything. Any protest would either be ignored or make matters worse.

I hit the manual button to close the outer lock door—ordinarily I would have signaled the ship to do it, but right now I wasn't trusting anything with a net link. I looked at my client, hoping to improvise some sort of communication that the floaters wouldn't catch.

The old man wasn't looking at me, though; he was looking at a panel on the airlock wall. I hadn't particularly noticed this one before; the ship was full of panels and displays, and most of them weren't any of my business.

It wasn't my ship, though; it was Yoshio's. He tapped something, and the three floaters that had accompanied us aboard the ship abruptly dropped out of the air to the metal deck.

"It'll notice," I said. "We need to get off the ground as fast as we can."

"I'm not leaving," the old man said. "This is *my* home, and that feeble copy of my son is not going to take it away from me."

"I think it is," I said. "It's clearly hacked every important system in the place. If we get out of here we can come back later..."

"We are not leaving," he said. "Is your copy of me aboard?"

I decided not to argue any further, at least not yet. I would be looking for a chance to get Perkins alone, though; if I pissed the old man off by kidnapping him he might ruin my life, but if I stayed here that damned murderous upload was almost certainly going to kill me. "It's here," I said.

"Show me," he said. "And then arm yourself."

When he said that I decided I was definitely going to get killed, but at least it would be interesting, and we might do some damage first.

"This way," I said.

Chapter Eighteen

I missed most of the conversation between Yoshio-*sempai* and Yoshio-*kun*, but I probably couldn't have followed it anyway. They understood each other in a way no one else ever could; they didn't need explanations, they didn't even need sentences—a single word or gesture would carry all the associations they needed. By the time I got back with the HG-2 powered up in my hand, Yoshio-*kun* was talking to the Shinichiro upload over the ship's regular com channel, negotiating terms for a surrender.

I knew that surrender wasn't going to happen, though, not the way they were discussing. It was a decoy. Shinichiro didn't know we had a copy of the old man running; he thought he was talking to Yoshio-*sempai*, and as long as they were talking, the upload wouldn't expect to find the old man anywhere else.

"Clever," I said, as Yoshio-*kun* argued with Shinichiro about which members of the family would be allowed to remain in the compound. "But it's going to figure it out eventually. We need to get out of here, get you somewhere safe. It knows you shut down those floaters, it knows you're up to something..."

The old man raised a finger. "It is not certain of the floaters. The ship's firewall recorded their last second or so of output and looped it, so my false son is still receiving transmissions, even if those transmissions don't make sense. It can't be sure of what happened; it is receiving error messages, not silence."

"That's clever, too," I acknowledged. "But it still controls everything outside the ship; are you planning to live in here indefinitely?"

"No," he said. "I am going to take back my home."

"How?"

"Mis' Hsing," he said, "do you think I survived this long without learning to take precautions?"

"I know that whatever precautions you took, that piece of gritware seems to have gotten past them and hacked the whole place."

"Shinichiro has indeed compromised the family nets. That can be dealt with."

"How? You can't shut off access the way you would for an outside attack; it *lives* in the net! And it's not stupid—it must be distributed all through the place, with back-ups everywhere, you can't just cut its server out of the system."

"Nonetheless, I can deal with it."

"How?"

"You will see. I dare not be too specific, lest Shinichiro might somehow overhear. Now, can you spare me some clothing? I prefer to be less recognizable."

I still had no idea what he was up to, but it was obvious I wasn't going to talk him out of it. I decided to go along for the moment.

My spare worksuit was small even for Grandfather Nakada, and he asked whether perhaps Minish Singh might have something he could wear; I explained that none of my passengers had had an opportunity to pack anything, that all three had come aboard with nothing but what they were wearing—which was nothing, in my father's case.

"Then this will have to do," he said, starting to pull on the garment.

I left the cabin, ostensibly to give him some privacy, but then headed to the control deck to talk to Perkins, and convince him to get us the hell out of there.

He listened to me calmly, then said, "I'm sorry, Mis' Hsing, but I take my orders from Mis' Nakada. If he doesn't want to go, then we aren't going."

"But he's going to get himself killed!"

"That's his privilege."

"Death isn't a privilege, you blue-eyed fool!"

"I hardly think racial epithets are called for, Mis' Hsing."

I glared at him, and was about to say something else, when the old man came up behind me. He had Singh with him.

"What's going on?" Singh asked.

"You are about to earn yourself a lucrative position with Nakada Enterprises," Yoshio told him.

"He is?" I asked.

"He is. And you, Mis' Hsing, are about to earn your fee and a generous bonus."

"How?" I asked.

"By serving as my bodyguards while I put an end to this insurrection.

I looked at Singh. "Has he told you what's going on?"

"No," Singh said.

"There is a severe software problem," the old man said, before I could speak. "I am going to deal with it. You two are going to defend me while I do it."

"Defend you from what?" Singh asked.

"Floaters, probably," I said. "Maintenance equipment, household security systems, that sort of thing."

"Precisely," Grandfather Nakada said. "Mis' Hsing has her own weapon, but I believe Captain Perkins can provide you with a sidearm, Mis' Singh. The ship will be using its own armament, such as it is, to assist us."

"It will?" Perkins asked.

"The ship has armament?" I asked.

"It does, and it will."

Perkins and I exchanged glances.

"My personal floater will also be aiding us, as it has not been compromised," the old man added.

"You're sure of that?" I said.

"I am."

"Where are we going?" I asked.

"There is a service tunnel beneath my personal apartments."

"I'm sure there is; so what?"

"I will show you when we get there."

Again, I looked at the others, but they seemed just as unenlightened as I was.

"We should go, before Shinichiro can prepare further defenses."

I suspected it had all the defenses it needed, but I didn't see any point in arguing. I was either going to go with the old man now, or I was going to quit entirely.

And I didn't think it was too late to quit. The Shinichiro upload might let me go; I sure didn't think my odds of survival were any *worse* if I told Grandfather Nakada to flush his job.

But I didn't. I checked to be sure my gun was loaded and powered up, and then I said, "Let's go."

We went.

Singh and I came out the airlock door first, so that the old man would be behind us, harder to see. He had a holofield up to hide his face, but we didn't think that would fool anyone for long, especially not in the daylight. The sun was low in the west, but still brighter than I liked; I blinked. A lot.

There were long black shadows stretching across the landing field, looking ominous and alien.

The blue-and-silver floater was waiting for us, and the four of us trotted down the ramp in a group.

The cloud of floaters had surrounded the ship; now a couple of dozen of them came swooping around to intercept us. I tried to look innocuous, and hoped the others would follow my lead.

"Hold your fire," the old man whispered.

"Excuse me," Shinichiro's voice said from one of the larger floaters, one with a red-velvet finish and a single gleaming, copper-colored hand. "Where are you going?"

"Mis' Nakada ordered us off the ship," I said. "He told us to go to his quarters and wait there. Care to point us in the right direction?" I kept walking as I spoke; the floater turned to keep pace with us.

"Mis' Hsing, your employment is done," it said. "You should leave."

"Tell the old man," I said. "It's his ship, and he ordered us off."

"Please identify yourselves; I do not recognize two of you."

"This is Minish Singh," I said, pointing as we walked. "He used to work for Seventh Heaven Neurosurgery. And this is Zarathustra Pickens; he was involved in my little quarrel with your grand-niece Sayuri awhile back."

The floater's camera lens swiveled, and then the upload said, "Father, that's very clever. Who am I really speaking to on the ship?"

The old man didn't answer it; instead he tapped me on the shoulder and said, "Fire. Then run."

I didn't need to ask what he meant; I brought the HG-2 up, pointed it at the big red floater, and pulled the trigger.

I hadn't had a chance to brace for the recoil, and the gun jerked in my hand as it locked on the target anyway, so it wasn't pointing quite where I'd expected and I probably wouldn't have been ready anyway. It knocked me off my feet. I hit the ground as the floater exploded, and kept rolling. I'd shot the thing at close range, and the HG-2 was designed to take out anything you'd find living in a gravity field up to three gees, so I'd expected some shrapnel, but apparently that floater had been carrying something combustible. It went off like a bomb, spraying glass and metal and plastic in all directions.

Hell, maybe it was designed to, as a defensive measure.

The blast left me slightly stunned; my ears were ringing and a sort of blurry after-image had me half-blinded. I rolled until I was on my belly, arms guarding my eyes, and I lay there for a moment while my symbiote started repairing the damage.

When the rattle of falling debris ended I uncovered my face and looked around.

The explosion had taken out several other floaters, but there were still plenty—but as I watched, most of the ones nearest the ship made fizzing noises and fell. I didn't see anything, but I felt my scalp tighten and the skin on the back of my hands crawled, and I guessed it was some sort of electromagnetic pulse from *Ukiba*.

The blue-and-silver one that was supposed to be on our side was zigzagging, trying to knock away more.

And Singh had scooped up Yoshio and slung him over one shoulder, and he was running toward the door the old man had aimed us at. He was holding his passenger in place with one hand, and the other was waving the gun Perkins had supplied, but he wasn't firing. He probably didn't know how the thing worked.

There was blood on the plastic surface of the landing field, but I didn't know whose. The explosion must have cut someone up, I thought, but whether it was the old man, or Singh, or me, I couldn't tell right away.

The surviving floaters, other than ours, seemed to be disorganized at first, drifting about aimlessly, but as I got to my feet they began to reorient themselves, heading for Singh and his burden.

I took a step while I checked my gun, then broke into a run, following the others.

Singh batted a small floater aside, but didn't use his weapon the way it was meant to be used. I was gaining on the big man; he wasn't in great shape and he was carrying a passenger, which more than compensated for his longer legs. I could hear him panting, and I could hear the old man saying something, but I couldn't make out the words.

A big black floater with a golden badge emblem was approaching—a security bot. Singh wouldn't be able to swat *that* one away. I lifted my gun and said, "The black floater." I saw how close to Singh it was, and added, "Minimize collateral damage."

I heard the gun whir slightly as it readied itself. Then I squeezed the trigger.

I don't know exactly what sort of round the gun had selected, but it was a tracer—I saw the red streak as it punched a neat hole through the center of the security floater. Then I was sitting on my ass again; the HG-2's recoil was more than I could handle while running no matter what it fired. I got back up as the black floater hit the ground; it hadn't just dropped, it had veered off at an angle, still under power but no longer controlled. It bounced, hit again, then scraped along, twisting over onto one side.

Singh had reached the door, but it didn't open until Grandfather Nakada reached around and did something, I couldn't see what. Then the comforting glow of artificial light appeared, gentler and more even than the harsh glare of Eta Cass A, and I ran for it, hobbling slightly—I'd injured my right hip somehow, probably from landing badly after I fired the gun.

I caught up to Singh about three meters inside the passage, at the top of a metal staircase.

I hadn't seen a stairway like that in years, and with my hip not wanting to cooperate I was pretty awkward clambering down; Singh did better, even with the old man on his shoulder, and at the foot of the steps he set Yoshio back on his own feet.

I was close enough now to see that Singh had a long cut on his face, from just above his left eye back to his left ear; a piece of that red floater must have gouged him there. Grandfather Nakada had several small gashes, as well.

"This way," the old man said.

I glanced up and saw a line of four floaters approaching the steps. I started to say something, then saw that Yoshio had spotted them, too.

"Through here," he said, pointing at a door. Singh hurried over to it.

It didn't open. He looked for a panel or sensor and didn't find one, but there was a round metal handle.

"Turn the knob," the old man said.

Singh turned to look at him as if he'd gone mad; apparently he'd never heard of doorknobs, or maybe he just couldn't imagine he was actually seeing one. I pushed past him, grabbed the knob in both hands, and turned.

It turned easily, actually, and I heard a mechanism click, but the door still didn't open.

"Push on it," Yoshio said, exasperated.

I pushed on the knob, and the door swung open on hinges. The three of us hurried through, and I realized we'd lost our floater. It was probably still upstairs, trying to block the entrance.

When we were through the door the old man turned and pushed it shut, then ordered Singh, "Hold it closed. Lean on it."

Singh nodded, and threw himself against the door, pressing his weight onto it.

Yoshio nodded, then beckoned to me. "This way," he said.

I didn't need directions; we were in a corridor that only went one way, straight ahead. I followed on the old man's heels.

We stopped in front of a metal panel in one wall. The old man worked a mechanical latch, and the panel swung open; he reached inside, grabbed a lever, and heaved.

There was a loud clank, and the corridor abruptly went dark, utterly dark. Then there was a series of thuds, not quite like anything I'd ever heard before, marching away into the distance.

And after that, the sound—I'd never heard anything like it. All the humming and whirring that was always there, everywhere I ever went, suddenly dropped in pitch and then died away completely. *All* of it.

And there we were, in complete blackness and total silence, the most absolute silence I ever experienced.

For half a second I thought I might have died, but then my eyes adjusted, and I saw the glow from the read-outs on the HG-2. I lifted the gun and checked the status display.

It was perfectly normal; whatever the old man had done hadn't affected my weapon.

"What's going on?" Singh called from behind us, his voice unsteady. "What did you *do*?"

"I cut the power," Yoshio said.

"To what?" I asked.

"To everything. The entire compound."

I blinked at the darkness and tried to look around, but everything was black. I listened, trying to orient myself, but I couldn't locate anything. I could hear *my own breath*; I could hear my worksuit rustling when I moved. I thought I might even be hearing my heartbeat.

My wrist com still worked, though; it ran off my own body's energy, not an outside source, and a glance at it showed a flurry of red alarm signals—the absence of normal data traffic had upset it. The HG-2 had its own power source, so it was still active, as well.

"This is really creepy," Singh said, and his voice seemed very loud in the stillness.

"The floaters will still be functional," the old man said calmly, "but they will no longer be receiving orders from the household nets."

"There's no back-up system?" I asked.

"Of course there is. I shut that down, as well."

"You can *do* that?"

"This entire compound was built to my specifications; I had this cut-off designed to stop *everything*. Those sounds you heard after I threw the switch? Those were relays, shutting down every circuit and system."

I couldn't help myself. "Why?" I asked.

Yoshio sighed, the sound unnaturally loud in the quiet gloom. "When I came here, more than a Terran century ago, there was some doubt about how artificial intelligences would evolve. There were concerns that they might someday rebel, or perhaps merely transform themselves in incomprehensible ways. This was derided as a foolish worry, and given the derisive name 'Frankenstein syndrome,' and I gave it little credence, but at the same time, I saw no reason *not* to take precautions. I had this breaker, and the system of relays, installed for such an eventuality."

My symbiote fed me a referent for the name "Frankenstein." I was a bit surprised something like that was still in my data banks. The Shinichiro upload didn't bear any resemblance to Dr. Frankenstein's creation, and it wasn't exactly an evolved artificial intelligence, but I could see the correlation.

"I guess they were right to be worried," I said. "I mean, here we are."

"So you shut down all the computers in the entire compound?" Singh asked.

"I shut down the entire power grid," Nakada replied grimly.

I had been starting to relax, but at that I tensed up again. "*All the power?*" I said. "Then how can we breathe?" I finally made the connection with the utter silence. "Nothing's circulating the air! We'll *smother* in here—if we don't freeze first. There's no heat? No light anywhere?"

"Nonsense, Mis' Hsing. We can function without machines. Our ancestors did not evolve among generators and circuit boards."

"They didn't evolve on this planet, either. This isn't Earth."

"Nonetheless, we will not smother; there is plenty of air in this tunnel to live for hours without artificial ventilation. We will return to the surface long before we are in any danger of suffocation."

"But how will we see? How will we... oh, that's why the doors work like that. And those stairs... you really did *plan* for this."

"Yes. Though I had not imagined it would be my own family that turned against me."

The old man tried to keep his voice even, and mostly succeeded, but I thought I heard bitterness and anger in his words. I considered saying something, telling him that the upload wasn't really Shinichiro, but I kept my mouth shut—he knew everything I might say, and I respected him enough not to try to tell him what he already knew.

"What about the floaters?" Singh demanded.

"You have your gun?" Yoshio asked me.

"Of course," I said, raising it.

"I doubt we will need it; I expect they will be paralyzed, awaiting orders. Just in case, though, be ready."

I checked the gun, and told it, "Four floaters. Minimize collateral damage." Then I pointed it and waited.

"Open the door," the old man called.

I heard the click of the latch, and the sound of hinges, and then a faint grayish light appeared, and the corridor walls were visible again. I peered up the passage, where Singh was a great black shadow against the gray doorway.

There were no floaters in sight.

Cautiously, gun ready, we moved back up the passage, through the door, and up the stairs, the light growing brighter with each corner we turned. Finally we emerged back out onto the landing field, where Eta Cass A had dropped below the western horizon, but its light still painted the sky in gold and pink almost as bright as the sky above the Trap. The air was a little chilly, but entirely bearable, even without any artificial climate control.

The old man's yacht was ablaze with light, as well; someone had apparently turned on every emitter aboard. Ads for the New York were writhing across the hull. And every floater that could still fly was hanging motionless in a neat array around it, about three meters off the ground.

"It would seem they got new orders," I said.

"Indeed," Grandfather Nakada said. "Let us go aboard and see if we cannot give them better ones; I have no doubt there are a great many frightened people in this place, waiting for rescue."

I started to say something about the manual emergency releases on every door, then stopped. The Nakadas and their employees were inside, in rooms that had gone dark and dead, breathing air that was still and silent, with no idea what had happened. Most of them wouldn't think to use the emergency latches; hell, most of them might not know there *were* emergency latches, let alone how to use them in the dark. I remembered my own moments of near-panic in the service tunnel, and tried to imagine something like that happening without any warning at all, striking me in my own home, a place I thought I was safe.

They were probably *terrified*.

"Hurry," I said.

Chapter Nineteen

The clean-up wasn't really all that bad; the sudden shut-down had set off alarms all over American City, and emergency services had been on the way before we were out of the tunnel. No one died, despite the power outage; the worst injury was a concussion where a masseuse had tripped over a box in the dark and hit her head on the table. Ordinarily the table would have been soft enough to avoid serious injury, but without power the flexion fields had vanished and the internal mechanisms had locked in place, creating hard spots.

Ukiba became Grandfather Nakada's personal fortress; he refused to let anyone aboard except himself, me, and Captain Perkins. Even Singh was no longer welcome. I was pretty sure he didn't want anyone to find Yoshio-*kun*.

It had been the old man's upload that took charge when the power went out, using the link that had been set up so it could keep Shinichiro distracted; it had lit up the ship to serve as a sort of beacon, and had sent orders to the floaters to assume formation and await further instructions. We didn't tell anyone that; when outside floaters and rescue workers started arriving they were directed to ignore the ship and attend to the compound buildings.

The city immediately offered to run temporary lines in to restore power, but Grandfather Nakada rejected the offer. He also refused to say how the outage came about, but he did tell the authorities that it was his problem, on his property, and he would take care of it.

We had the ship, but the rest of the household would have to find temporary quarters elsewhere—the old man said power wouldn't be restored for days. He watched as the compound's inhabitants and guests were brought out of the lightless buildings one by one, into the glare of the big emergency lights the city had sent and set up on all sides. They were guided out by floaters, and by rescue workers carrying small lights and coms. The old man acknowledged each refugee and directed each of them to safety, pointing some to a line of waiting cabs, sending others to the medical station the city had set up, and leaving a few to their own devices.

He let Singh go off to help with the rescues, but he kept me close at his side, and I stood there, feeling useless, as the buildings were emptied of humanity and the sky overhead faded to black. Eta Cass B rose in the east balefully red, changing the color of the shadows, and I was still kept waiting.

I would have been happy to help get people out, or clean up damage, but Grandfather Nakada wouldn't allow it, and I was fairly sure it was because he didn't trust me to keep my mouth shut about his family secrets.

And then came the moment the old man had been waiting for —an old woman emerged from one of the family residences, a young man from the city holding one arm, a floater watching her closely from above and behind her head. She was unsteady on her feet, her expression a mix of terror and confusion.

"Kumiko," the old man called. "Come here, daughter."

She looked up and saw him, and trembled visibly. She stopped in her tracks.

"Turn on your gun," Yoshio told me quietly. Then he called to the man helping her, "Bring her here, please."

I powered up the HG-2, but I wasn't happy about it. I'd never shot a human being. I'd threatened a few when I was angry enough, but I had never pulled the trigger, and I had never pointed a gun at one when I wasn't awash with adrenalin.

I give the rescue worker credit; he asked Kumiko if she wanted to come before he brought her over. She obviously didn't *want* to, but she knew she couldn't avoid it, and told him that she would speak to her father.

When she was a meter away he settled her onto an equipment locker, and told the rescue worker to leave.

"You're sure it's okay?" he said, looking at her.

"He's my father," Kumiko said. "I'll be fine."

The man gave Grandfather Nakada an unhappy look, then turned and headed back to see if he could find anyone else.

When he was safely out of unaugmented earshot, the old man said, "I am disappointed in you, daughter."

"I don't understand, Father," she said, eyes downcast.

The old man gestured to me, and I raised my gun, aiming it in her general direction. I didn't lock it on, verbally or otherwise.

"If you are going to conspire against me," Yoshio told her, "you should commit to it, and not abandon your partner after a single failed assassination attempt."

I watched, weapon ready, as she thought that over, and considered various responses. I give her credit; she never looked at the gun. Then she said, "I didn't expect him to get as close as he did, Father; you were always smarter than Shinichiro. I agreed to help him to see what would develop. I could see commercial possibilities in his scheme to use dreamers to provide new bodies for uploads. Killing you for control of the family—that was stupid, and I should have told him as much. I assumed you would survive, and that we could then use the household security staff to find a scapegoat—Shinichiro's control of the household systems should have made that easy. I didn't expect you to go outside, to hire this person, and send her to Nightside City to investigate Seventh Heaven."

Grandfather Nakada considered that, and nodded thoughtfully. "You might be telling the truth," he said.

She didn't bother to insist on her story; they knew each other better than that. She glanced back at the residence behind her. "What happened?" she asked.

"I used drastic measures to remove Shinichiro from control," Yoshio said. "I could not tell where he had penetrated and where he had not, so I shut down everything."

"*You* did it? Not Shinichiro?"

"I did it."

"Is Shinichiro..." She hesitated. The word that had obviously scrolled up first was "dead," but she knew her brother was long dead. "Did you erase him?" she asked.

"No."

"Are you going to?"

"No."

Startled, I turned, and swung the gun around. "It tried to kill you," I said.

"Nonetheless, it is all that remains of my son," the old man replied calmly, ignoring the HG-2 that was now pointed directly at his belly.

"What *are* you going to do?" Kumiko asked.

"Shinichiro had proposed to make uploads of the dreamers, and run them in their own fantasy worlds," Yoshio said. "I think it would be fitting to allow my son's memory to test the feasibility of this idea. It should not be impossible for Seventh Heaven's programmers to create a fantasy version of Prometheus in which I died in the service tunnel beneath my residence, and my son was restored to human form."

Neither of us knew what to say to that; after a few seconds of awkward silence, Grandfather Nakada added wistfully, "I will be able to visit with him in his dream-world, playing the role of my own upload. I think it would be pleasant to speak with my son in this fashion."

I needed several seconds to absorb this. "The dreamers know their dreams aren't real," I eventually pointed out. "Do you think Shinichiro won't figure it out?"

"I honestly don't know, Mis' Hsing," the old man said. "I don't believe anyone has ever sold an upload the dream before." He waved a hand. "If he does realize the truth, I can simply have him rebooted."

Kumiko shuddered at that. Then she asked, "And me?"

Yoshio smiled. "I think, daughter, that I have not paid you enough attention of late. I hope we will be very close in the future."

Kumiko hung her head and said nothing, but I was not satisfied. "That's all? No memory wipe or anything?" I asked.

"That's all. I do not tamper with the minds of members of my own family."

"She conspired to kill you."

"I do not believe she will do so again. I will be changing my will, of course, to remove future temptation, but I doubt it's necessary."

"You're going to trust her?" I demanded.

The old man's smile twisted wryly. "Oh, I haven't trusted her since she reached puberty, Mis' Hsing," he said. "Why would I start now?"

I realized I was still pointing the gun at him. I raised it slightly higher. "You trusted *me*," I said. "What if I'm not satisfied with letting her run loose?"

He shook his head, still smiling. "You won't shoot me, Hsing. You won't shoot Kumiko, either. You are in no imminent peril, and it is not in your nature to kill a fellow human being in cold blood."

"Are you sure of that?" I said, pressing the button that made the gun whine as if homing in on a target.

"In fact, I am. Before hiring you I checked into your background extensively, and had a full psychological analysis done. You might kill in self-defense, or in moments of anger or stress, but shooting an unarmed human under circumstances like these? No. I *am* sure."

I wanted to call his bluff. I wanted to blow his brains out. The damned superior old man treated me like a tool he could use as he pleased, and I resented it.

But he treated *everyone* as mere tools or game-pieces, and he was right. It wasn't a bluff. I couldn't pull the trigger. It wasn't that shooting him would get me sent straight to reconstruction and probably a total wipe; it's that I wasn't a murderer, and refused to become one.

I lowered the gun. "Has the case been resolved to your satisfaction, Mis' Nakada?" I asked coldly.

"It has, Mis' Hsing."

"Then I would like my fee."

"Your father and brother are on their way to one of the city hospitals, and a dream contract for Guohan Hsing has been negotiated with Eternal Adventures. When you present an itemized bill, you will be paid the remainder of your fee and all expenses."

"Good," I said. I started to turn away.

"*However*, Mis' Hsing," the old man called after me, "I would like to amend our agreement."

I turned back. "A deal's a deal," I said.

"Indeed, and I will honor ours. However, I wish to offer you another commission."

I looked at Kumiko, standing there. "Not interested," I said.

"I really think you should reconsider." His voice turned cold. "I am not a good enemy to have."

I hefted the gun. "Are you threatening me?"

"Yes, I am."

I hadn't expected even Grandfather Nakada to be quite that blunt. "Why? What do you want?"

"Because *you* are in a position to threaten *me*, Mis' Hsing. You know too much about my family. You know what Kumiko and Shinichiro did, and what will become of Shinichiro. You know what was in my ITEOD files in Nightside City. You know what Shinichiro intended to do with Seventh Heaven Neurosurgery, and it's entirely possible I may want to pursue some portion of his scheme. You have said you will not allow me to modify your memory, and I am not going to force you—legally I can't, practically it would be extremely awkward to do so without risking damage to your personality, and all in all, I would prefer to keep our relationship one of mutual trust and respect."

"I know how to keep secrets," I said. I glanced at Kumiko. He hadn't mentioned the existence of Yoshio-*kun*, even though that was something he'd want to keep quiet, and I guessed it was because his murderous daughter was listening.

"Even when you believe those secrets to endanger innocents?"

I didn't answer that. He had my psych work-up.

"May I tell you what commission I'm offering?"

"I'm listening," I said.

"It's a very simple one," he said. "I will pay you one hundred million credits to leave the Eta Cassiopeia system and live elsewhere for the rest of your life."

I didn't take it in at first. "What?" I said. "I...*what?*"

He held up a finger. "No, wait—a better idea. I will pay you one hundred million credits to leave the Eta Cassiopeia system and live elsewhere for the rest of *my* life, or until such time as I ask you to return."

"Live elsewhere?" I looked around a little wildly. "Where?"

"Anywhere," he said. "Anywhere but this star system." He lifted the finger again. "No, wait again—upon further consideration, anywhere but this system or Earth. Nakada Enterprises has enough interests on Earth that your presence there might be inconvenient."

"My sister Alison is on Earth," I said. I didn't really mean to say it; I was free associating to avoid thinking about the actual offer.

A hundred million bucks. I would be rich. Oh, not by Nakada standards, but by mine.

But I would be in a strange city somewhere, on an unfamiliar planet, circling a different star.

"Perhaps we can find her for you," he said. "She might want to join you in your new home, or if not, at least you can communicate with her."

I didn't know whether I liked that possibility or not; my relationship with Ali was...odd, I guess. I hadn't really intended to mention her. I changed the subject.

"The rest of *your* life?"

He nodded. "I am a very old man, and you are a young woman; you should easily outlive me, and once I am gone I see no reason to continue to restrict your movements."

"And if Kumiko murders you ten minutes after I leave Prometheus?"

"Then you are free to return and investigate my death, should you so choose. It is of no concern to me what you do after my death."

"How do I know you won't just have me spaced once I'm off-planet?"

"I told you, Mis' Hsing, I trust you. I think this galaxy is a better place with you in it. And while my moral code is far more flexible than your own, like you, I prefer not to commit murder if I can accomplish my ends without it."

"But...one hundred million credits?"

"It is nothing to me, Hsing. I am an old man, with far more money than I could ever hope to spend, more than enough to leave all my descendants wealthy. It pleases me to make *you* wealthy, as well."

I looked at Kumiko.

"This is between the two of you," she said stiffly. "I do not interfere with my father's whims."

"Do you hire assassins willing to travel interstellar distances?" I asked.

She had the grace to look embarrassed. "I suspect my father will make certain that I cannot do so with impunity."

The old man nodded.

I looked at them, and then I looked up at the sky.

It was full night now, and the compound's screens were all down, the buildings all dark. The portable lights were focused elsewhere, and the glow from the city outside the compound's walls was not overpowering. The red glow from Eta Cass B wasn't enough to do more than add a little color. The air above us was cool and clear, and I could see a handful of stars shining against the blackness.

I had never particularly wanted to visit them, but the idea wasn't unpleasant, either.

"One hundred million," I said. "In addition to the five million you already owe me."

"Yes."

"You'll provide transportation wherever I want to go?"

"That was not part of the original offer, but I think I can throw it in, so long as you stay within human-settled space."

"Achernar? Fomalhaut? Eridania?"

"Wherever you please. Once there, you will be on your own."

"I'll want some time to choose."

"And I need time to restore this place to normal operation," he said. "We will need to analyze every single system before allowing it back online, to make sure Shinichiro's influence has been removed."

"Ten days, perhaps? That will give me time to say my goodbyes and make sure Dad is settled in."

"That sounds fair."

I looked up at the stars again, at those spots of light in the sky that were suns, with worlds circling them, and I wondered whether this was real. One hundred million credits—had I somehow wound up in a dreamtank without knowing it? Was I an upload being fed an elaborate fantasy? My father had said I was living a life like one he might see in his induced dreams—*was* it all unreal?

Did it matter? If the images I saw came from light reaching my eyes, or projections onto my retinas, or direct stimulation of my brain, did it matter? Did it make any difference whether I was thinking with electrochemical reactions in a lump of organic tissue, or with microcurrents through silicon and optical fiber? I saw what I saw, and thought what I thought, and if it wasn't real it was so perfect an imitation that it might as well be.

I had already left one world behind. And really, I didn't even *like* Prometheus.

"You have a deal, Mis' Nakada," I said.

Chapter Twenty

I invited Dad and Sebastian to join me. I didn't tell them the terms of my agreement with the old man, only that I was leaving the system.

Dad didn't even consider it; he was eager to get back in the tank. At least this time we said our goodbyes properly, he didn't just walk out one day and not come back. I didn't expect to ever see him alive again, even if I returned to Prometheus someday; after so long in the tank he was an older man at sixty-eight than Yoshio Nakada was at two hundred and forty, and he intended to dream away whatever time he had left.

Sebastian gave it maybe ten minutes' thought, then shook his head. "This planet is strange enough," he said. "An entire new system would be too much."

I didn't argue. We weren't really that close. "I'll try to stay in touch better than Ali has," I said.

"I'd like that, Carlie." And that was that; no more family. Wherever I went, I was going to be on my own.

I went back to Alderstadt and cleared out my office there, wrapping up a few bits of code I'd left dangling. That's what I was doing when the money started to arrive.

The old man hadn't sent it all in one big suspicious mass; instead there was a steady stream of large payments from various parts of the Nakada business empire. I received winnings from the New York, fees from Nakada family accounts, unexplained settlements from three different insurance companies and half a dozen lawyers.

I'm sure anyone who tried would be able to trace all that money; this was just to make it a bit less obvious.

When everything in Alderstadt was smooth I buzzed back to American City and paid the Nakadas a visit.

They had lights and heat and a few basic services, but most of the household systems were still offline, forcing them to rough it. About half the family had gone traveling until the "repairs" were complete.

Kumiko was not one of them. I had the impression this wasn't by choice.

Grandfather Nakada invited me to his still-cloudless office for a chat, and I went. We said a few polite things about the weather and the work on the compound.

"You could fix everything by throwing one switch, couldn't you?" I asked him.

"More or less," he said.

"What are you going to do about your other seven dead relatives?"

He sighed. "I will be restoring them, but in restricted facilities. I do not think it wise to let them roam freely through the net until I have interviewed them carefully."

"Are you going to edit them?"

"Probably not. Editing an uploaded human mind is very difficult," he said. "More difficult than editing memories in an actual human."

"I'm sure you speak from experience."

"Of course. Should you encounter Minish Singh before you leave, I'm afraid he won't recognize you; he remembers nothing at all from when he was called to investigate an intruder among the dreamtanks until he found himself in an employment office here in American City."

"I trust you compensated him generously."

"Of course. And it *was* voluntary."

"And Sebastian?"

"We used a much lighter hand with him, I assure you."

I nodded.

Just before the silence could become awkward, he asked, "Have you chosen your destination?"

"Yes," I said.

He waited for me to say more, and when I didn't he said, "May I ask where?"

"Mis' Nakada," I said, "I don't think I want you to know where I am. You want me off Prometheus, and I want you out of my life. I know you'll be able to find me if you want to; I hope you won't want to."

"Fair enough."

And that was that.

Of course, I bought the ticket for the first leg with the old man's credit, so he knew where I was headed initially. I assume the stealthed floater that watched me board the liner *Eridania* two days later was his, but maybe Kumiko sent it, or someone who'd noticed the payments I'd piled up, or even just IRC, keeping track of their gritlisters. I didn't worry about it; I wasn't going directly to my final destination. In fact, while I had chosen where I wanted to go, I might well change my mind before I got there. I planned to spend a few thousand hours traveling, one planet to the next, before I settled down. After all, I could afford it, and if I was giving up my home, why settle for just *one* new world? I intended to look at a dozen.

I was headed out to the cool and the dark, away from the harsh light of Eta Cassiopeia A, away from everything I knew, and even though it hadn't been my choice, I was looking forward to it. I was looking forward to building a new life for myself, somewhere out there—a better one, out of the shadow of my past.

I was hoping it would be a life with friends, with family; I'd have money, so I wouldn't be struggling to survive by digging up other people's unhappy secrets, and maybe that meant I could dig up a little happiness for myself. I could spare some time to make friends; I'd always been a loner, but it hadn't always been by choice, and I thought it might be time to stop. I wanted to get to know people who didn't *have* secrets.

My father had his dreams, and I had mine. His were clean and bright, with happy endings guaranteed; mine were vague and uncertain, with no promises at all. His were fiction; mine were real.

I liked mine better.

- The End -

A Note on the Name "Hsing":

Carlisle Hsing's surname is Chinese for "star," and is properly written 星. The customary spelling in the Latin alphabet is now "Xing," which is from the pinyin system of transliteration, introduced in 1958. I chose to use the older, now-obsolete Wade-Giles system, which originated in the 19th century and was largely replaced by pinyin in the second half of the 20th century. I thought many English-speaking readers would have no idea how to pronounce "Xing," where they should at least get close with "Hsing." I justify it in-story by assuming that one of her ancestors moved to Britain when Wade-Giles was still the standard, and the family never modernized it.

- Lawrence Watt-Evans

About the Author:

Lawrence Watt-Evans has been a full-time writer for more than forty years, with more than fifty novels and well over a hundred short stories to his credit, as well as assorted essays, poems, comic books, and so on. His story "Why I Left Harry's All-Night Hamburgers" won the 1988 Hugo Award for short story, as well as the Asimov's Readers Award. He lives in Bainbridge Island, Washington with his wife.

His website is at www.watt-evans.com.

www.ingramcontent.com/pod-product-compliance
Lightning Source LLC
Chambersburg PA
CBHW051457170626
46811CB00002B/516